"Did you mean it about helping with Sophie?"

"Yes." Joella drew the word out as her brows slanted upward.

"The thing is, getting a handle on the ranch is taking all my concentration, and when Sophie needs attention, everything comes to a screeching halt and—" Stopping himself, Samuel shrugged. "Sorry, I've been a little overwhelmed."

"It's okay. I get it." Joella gnawed her lower lip. "Would it help if I came over for a couple of hours in the afternoons?"

He nearly collapsed with gratitude and relief. "You'd be saving my life."

"I could start tomorrow, say around two o'clock?"

An agreement reached, Joella said her goodbyes. As Samuel watched her from the window, he felt himself smile. They still weren't exactly *friends*, but something about Joella drew him in a way he'd never experienced.

Could she really believe he was still *that guy*? Years ago, when he'd never wrote or called after she'd returned home at the end of summer vacation, she must have been both confused and hurt.

Would anything convince her he'd changed?

Award-winning author **Myra Johnson** writes emotionally gripping stories about love, life and faith. She is a two-time finalist for the ACFW Carol Award and winner of the 2005 RWA Golden Heart® Award. Married since 1972, Myra and her husband have two married daughters and seven grandchildren. She and her husband reside in Texas, sharing their home with two pampered rescue dogs.

Books by Myra Johnson

Love Inspired

The Ranchers of Gabriel Bend

The Rancher's Family Secret
The Rebel's Return

Rancher for the Holidays
Her Hill Country Cowboy
Hill Country Reunion
The Rancher's Redemption
Their Christmas Prayer

Visit the Author Profile page at Harlequin.com.

The Rebel's Return

Myra Johnson

ISBN-13: 978-1-335-56751-2

The Rebel's Return

This edition published by arrangement with Harlequin Books S.A.

For questions and comments about the quality of this book, please contact us at CustomerService@Harlequin.com.

Love Inspired
22 Adelaide St. West, 41st Floor
Toronto, Ontario M5H 4E3, Canada
www.LoveInspired.com

Printed in U.S.A.

For God hath not given us the spirit of fear;
but of power, and of love, and of a sound mind.

—*2 Timothy* 1:7

A best friend is someone you know will be there for you no matter what life throws your way, and there's no better friend I could ask for in this life than my sister-in-law Judy. I love you!

Chapter One

"Good idea, Lois. Using one of your barns for the party makes a lot of sense—for several reasons." Sitting at Lois Navarro's kitchen table, Joella James jotted the information down in her notebook.

Earlier that week, when Lois had approached Joella about planning her father-in-law's ninetieth birthday celebration, Joella had been both surprised and grateful. Surprised, because Arturo Navarro hadn't fully resolved his longstanding bitterness toward the family of Joella's business partner Lindsey McClement Navarro. And grateful, because fledgling River Bend Events and Wedding Chapel, based at the McClement ranch, desperately needed to book more—and larger—events if they had any hope of keeping this venture afloat.

"The thing is..." Tugging on her salt-and-pepper braid, Lois cast a distracted glance toward the hallway. "When I first talked to you about doing the party, I didn't know my husband was going to get thrown from a horse the very next day and require a trip to the ER."

Joella had heard all about Hank Navarro's injuries—his leg broken in two places, a cracked rib and some serious bruising. She offered a concerned frown. "How's he doing?"

"He won't admit it, but he's in quite a bit of pain. And extremely grumpy about being out of commission—especially with foaling season coming up, one of our busiest times of the year."

"Won't Spencer be able to help?" Their son, who'd married Lindsey last weekend on Valentine's Day, was a top-notch horseman.

"I'm sure he'll do what he can, but he and Lindsey are barely back from their honeymoon. Besides, he has his rescue horses to take care of, and now he'll be helping Lindsey and Audra with their cattle." Audra McClement Forrester, Lindsey's widowed aunt, had been struggling to manage the ranch on her own until Lindsey's arrival last fall.

Horses, cattle, ranch life…it was a whole new experience for Joella since she'd left her corporate event planning job in Dallas and moved to the McClement ranch in the Texas

Hill Country. But it was exactly the fresh start she needed, a chance not only to escape the city but to put a nearly disastrous failure behind her. At least, she prayed it would stay in the past. She couldn't bear it if her issues followed her to Gabriel Bend and caused problems for Lindsey and their other business partner, caterer Holly Elliot. The three had been best friends since high school.

When Lois touched her hand, she startled. "Sorry, my mind was wandering."

"You looked a million miles away. Listen, I don't want you worrying about our situation. It'll all work out. We have a reliable foreman to oversee the stable hands, and Samuel has already said he'd come home to manage the office for as long as necessary."

"Samuel's moving back to the ranch?" A lump congealed in the pit of Joella's stomach.

"It took some coaxing, but he finally agreed. We're expecting him later today."

"That's…that's great." She'd been able to handle being around Spencer's identical twin brother last weekend for the wedding, but only because she'd stayed busy enough to keep her distance. No way would she succumb to his charms as she'd done that summer when they were teens. It didn't matter that her friends would love nothing better than to see her and

Samuel get together. It simply couldn't happen. Not with Samuel. Not with anyone.

"If he gets here early enough," Lois went on, "we'll bring him over with us for Spencer and Lindsey's welcome-home dinner this evening."

"No problem. Holly always cooks plenty." She scanned her notes. Best to steer this discussion back to party planning. "So we'll host the event in your barn, and I'll have Holly compile some menu suggestions for you to look over. Anything else I should—"

"Oh, he's here already." Lois jumped up from the table and started for the back door.

Swiveling toward the window, Joella glimpsed a flashy white SUV parking in the gravel driveway. Must be nice to be able to afford driving around in a Lexus. She almost felt sorry for all the women who'd be missing out over the next several weeks on the dates they could have had with tall, successful and handsomely bearded Samuel Navarro.

Then she noticed the ugly scratch running from his left front fender to the rear bumper. Whose heart had he broken to deserve getting keyed like that? He had seemed rather preoccupied last weekend, far removed from the impetuous, sociable teenage boy she remembered.

Well, no concern of hers. And no use delaying the inevitable. She tucked her notebook into her tote, then slipped on her sweater and followed Lois outside.

She stepped from the screen porch, her gaze meeting Samuel's as he emerged from his car. His eyes widened briefly in surprise before his mother demanded his full attention with a hug. Watching them, Joella sensed unease in Samuel's response. His smile seemed forced, his posture stiff.

With another concerned glance toward Joella, he backed out of his mother's embrace. "Mom, I need to tell you—"

A sound came from inside the car—*a baby's cry?* Mouth agape, Lois peered through the rear passenger window, then cast her son a confused stare. "Samuel? Whose baby is that?"

Eyelids falling shut, he dipped his chin. "She's mine. I didn't know how to explain over the phone."

It was Joella's turn to stare in disbelief. Torn between making a quiet departure or staying to see how the dropping of this bombshell played out, she found she couldn't move.

Samuel, a father? Memories of the summer when she was sixteen came roaring back. After returning home from two weeks spent with Lindsey at her grandparents' ranch—two weeks when Joella had experienced the biggest crush of her life on Samuel—she'd been terrified she'd also made the biggest mistake of her life. She'd never been more relieved when her worries had proved groundless.

Heart threatening to hammer out of her chest, she returned her attention to the man now lifting an infant from the back seat.

Of all the times to find Joella here. Samuel could see in her eyes the shock and disapproval. He'd hoped for a little more privacy when he introduced his family to Sophie—his baby girl, the daughter he hadn't known existed until eight days ago. How he'd managed to make it through his brother's wedding without totally losing it defied belief. Now he faced the task of explaining to his parents how all this had come about, and the last thing he needed was an audience.

Especially an audience containing Joella. Until the wedding, he hadn't seen her since they were teens. With her hair shimmering like gold beneath the twinkle lights that evening and the magenta velvet maid-of-honor gown swirling around her calves, she'd looked even more beautiful all grown up.

Did she recall their summer together all those years ago, or had time erased that memory? He'd always thought himself so suave and irresistible. But one night, he'd let things go a lot further than he'd ever intended.

Apparently, it was a lesson he hadn't learned the first time. Hence, the barely three-week-old baby he now attempted to quiet with gentle bounces against his shoulder. *Dear God, help! I have no idea what I'm doing!*

"Give her to me." Releasing a huff, Mom shifted Sophie into her arms. "There, there, sweet thing. Oh, your diaper's soaked through, and that's a hungry cry if I ever heard one." She hiked a brow at Samuel. "Don't just stand there. Get her things."

With a brisk nod and a stern mental shake, he retrieved Sophie's diaper bag from the back-seat floor. His mother slipped her arm through the strap and then strode to the house, pausing briefly to murmur something to Joella before continuing inside.

And leaving him out here alone with her? *Thanks a lot, Mom.*

Joella took a shaky breath. "You obviously have a lot to work out. I was just leaving anyway, so..." She turned toward the old barbed-wire fence separating the Navarro and McClement ranches. Then, abruptly, she swung around, head tilted and brown eyes simmering with accusation. "Not even a week ago, you stood next to your brother as his best man as if nothing had changed. How could you keep something like this a secret from your own family?"

All the doubt, confusion and frustration he'd kept bottled up since learning about Sophie came spewing out. "Believe me, no one was more stunned than I was." Exhaling sharply, he plowed his fingers through his hair while trying to regain some composure. "She was a secret even from me. I only learned about her the day before I came home for the wedding."

Brow furrowed, she looked temporarily taken aback. Then she stiffened, contempt filling her gaze. "What did you expect, playing the field the way you do? Don't think I haven't heard what a wild partier you became after leaving home."

The truth stung, even though he'd tried hard over the past several months to put his playboy life behind him. God knew his heart, even if he had a lot to prove to everyone else.

Right now, though, he was too overwhelmed and exhausted to defend himself. Sophie had been his for four days and four long, sleepless nights. If not for the temporary nanny the attorney had found for him after his ex-girlfriend, Chelsea Walford, signed over custody, he'd never have survived this long.

He lifted both hands in resignation. "Look, believe whatever you want. I've got enough on my plate just figuring out what happens next. Which, at the moment, is moving myself and my daughter into the apartment over the barn. So if you'll excuse me..."

He thumbed his key fob to open the back of his SUV. As he hauled out a suitcase, Joella's footsteps crunched across the gravel. A moment later, she disappeared around one of the barns, likely headed for the gap in the fence where the barbed wire had long ago been separated with a couple of cedar branches for easier passage—another reminder of the summer they'd spent together as teens.

He supposed he'd have to get used to seeing more of Joella now that she lived at the McClement ranch. Hopefully not any more than either of them was comfortable with.

He was still unloading luggage, boxes and infant supplies when his brother ambled over. He set aside a heavy cardboard carton to accept Spencer's bear hug. "What are you doing here, Spiny?" he asked, using his twin's childhood nickname. "Shouldn't you be with your beautiful wife?"

"Thought you might need some help moving in." Spencer thumped him on the back. "Good to have you home, Slam. Mom told me you'd be picking up the slack around here after Dad's accident. Thanks."

"Somebody had to, now that you're an old married man." They stepped apart, a weird kind of awkwardness momentarily silencing them. So much had changed lately, in both their lives. Samuel hefted the carton again. "Make yourself useful and grab something."

Just as his brother did so, the lid on Samuel's box popped open, and a small stuffed zebra fell out. Spencer stooped to retrieve it. "This looks familiar. Didn't you use to—" Glancing into the back of the SUV, he did a double take. "Wait—is that really a box of diapers? And a *portable crib*?"

Closing his eyes briefly, Samuel released a breath. "Let's go upstairs. I have a lot to tell you."

Minutes later, they sat opposite each other in the sparsely furnished living area. Samuel described the shocking phone call from the attorney, then showed Spencer the letter Chelsea had left for him:

Dear Samuel,

I've heard how hard you've been working to get your life back on track since you and I crashed and burned. I also know you're a believer who's become a kind, caring, godly man—the man you used to be before...well, everything.

The thing is, I can't see myself ever being a decent mom, not with my messed-up life. But you're so much stronger now, and you've got family to support you. So you're the only one I trust to raise this sweet baby girl.

I named her Sophie, which they say means wisdom, a quality I clearly lack and that she deserves. I know you'll be a great father to her. Someday, maybe you'll tell her I loved her enough to do this one good thing.

"Wow." Spencer whistled through his teeth as he laid the letter on the coffee table. "How are you handling this? Are you okay?"

"Not even close. But Sophie's depending on me, and I…" He shook his head in amazement. "I already love her so much. More than I ever imagined possible."

"And the mother—Chelsea? She really wants no part in the baby's life?"

"The attorney says she wants nothing at all from me except that I give Sophie a safe and loving home and be the best father I can be."

With God's help, he intended to do exactly that—another reason he'd known moving home to the ranch was the right thing. He couldn't bear the idea of a nanny raising his daughter while he dealt with the long hours and erratic schedule of commercial real-estate sales. Dad's accident, bad as it was, came as an opportunity to leave his old life in Houston behind. Here at home, he'd have his mom nearby to help and advise him.

"A baby," Spencer murmured. He palmed the back of his neck. "My brother's a dad. Which means I'm an uncle. Where is she? When can I meet her?"

"Mom commandeered her practically the moment we got here." Already missing his daughter, Samuel reached for the little zebra, cradling it with both hands. He'd selected it on the spur of the moment while shopping for baby gear because it reminded him of a favorite toy from his childhood.

Spencer's grin widened as he pushed to his feet. "Let's go see her right now. And you're bringing her over to the dinner, aren't you?"

Touched by his twin's enthusiasm, Samuel laughed. "I was going to, but…it just hit me how unfair this is. You and Lindsey should be the center of attention tonight. I should make my excuses and stay here with Sophie." *And avoid another uncomfortable encounter with Joella.*

"No way. I'm perfectly happy to share the spotlight. Besides," Spencer said with a groan,

"I'm ready to be done with all this wedding hoopla. If not for Dad's accident and needing to see to my horses, Lindsey and I would be heading back to the coast for another month or two of just the two of us."

Typical for his introverted twin. "The newness will wear off eventually. You can't blame the rest of us for being excited you and Lindsey are finally together."

A dreamy glint brightened Spencer's eyes. "I hope the newness of having Lindsey as my wife never wears off."

"Knowing you two, it won't." Samuel swallowed a pang of longing. If he'd stayed with Chelsea…

But no, not even a baby could have saved their volatile relationship. No doubt he'd deserved it, but he had her to thank for the six-foot-long scratch down the side of his car.

Fingertip to her chin, Joella surveyed the dining room table. She'd set places for nine—the newlyweds, Spencer's parents, Audra, Holly and her son Davey, and herself…plus Samuel. May as well get used to the idea of having him right next door. She didn't mind that Arturo wouldn't be joining them. Despite the fact that his grandson had married a McClement, the old man couldn't seem to release whatever grudge he held against Lindsey's late grandfather.

As Joella left the dining room, Spencer and Lindsey were just coming down the hall. Holding hands and laughing, they both startled when they saw her, and Lindsey's cheeks turned a riotous shade of pink.

Joella smirked and rolled her eyes. "Since we're all going to be living under the same roof indefinitely, you need to get over the 'blushing bride' thing."

"Don't count on it anytime soon," Lindsey said. "Can't help it when I'm married to the sweetest, kindest, most romantic guy alive."

"You left out best-looking," Spencer quipped, the faintest tinge of red blooming beneath his beard.

Lindsey poked him in the ribs. "In that case, it would be a tie with your identical twin brother." Turning serious, she continued, "I still can't believe Samuel has a baby. And how any mother could give her child away like that, I'll never understand."

Joella had fully intended to keep her nose out of Samuel's personal life, but Lindsey's remark caught her off guard. "What are you saying?"

"Spencer told me about the letter—"

Before Lindsey could complete her reply,

tires rumbled on the gravel driveway outside. Joella peered out the narrow entryway window to see Samuel's pearl-white Lexus come to a stop at the foot of the porch steps.

"Better go help." Spencer hurried down to the car, where he assisted his father from the passenger seat and handed him his crutches.

While he retrieved a wheelchair from the back, Samuel opened the rear door for his mother, who emerged with the baby in her arms. Reaching in behind her, Samuel hauled out an infant seat.

Lindsey rushed down the porch steps. "Finally! I've been dying to meet the newest addition to the Navarro family."

Joella moved out of the way as Spencer ushered his family inside and eased his dad into the wheelchair. Apparently hearing the commotion, Audra and Holly came in from the kitchen, nine-year-old Davey following close behind. All smiles, Lois quickly became the center of attention as she introduced her baby granddaughter.

A wild mix of emotions rooted Joella to the floor. It wasn't her place to judge either Samuel or the mother of his child, and yet she couldn't stop herself. A baby was both a blessing and a huge responsibility—a joy she could never allow herself to hope for. But if what Lindsey said was true, how could Samuel take this baby away from her mother instead of doing the right thing and marrying her so they could be the family their child deserved?

Samuel sidled over, hands in his pockets. "I know this is awkward. I told Spencer I'd stay home with the baby, but he wouldn't hear of it."

"I can see he's a very proud uncle. And obviously your mother is over the moon." Never mind about Hank, who looked supremely disgruntled. Whether his injuries were hurting him or he was upset about something else, Joella couldn't tell, but he was definitely keeping his distance from the adults crowding around to see the baby. "Excuse me. I need to check on...something."

Samuel followed her to the dining room. "Can I just apologize? I'm sorry all this got sprung on you today."

"Don't give it a second thought." She should at least try to be polite. Needlessly adjusting a place setting, she slid a glance in his direction. "Remind me—what's your daughter's name?"

"Sophie." His gaze drifted across the entryway to where his family had gathered in the living room. Awe in his voice, he repeated, "Her name's Sophie."

"It's a beautiful name." Thoughts darting,

she examined the table arrangement. "We don't have a high chair—must remember to add one or two to our event supplies. But I guess she's too little for one anyway."

"Yeah, it'll be a few months yet." Samuel snorted a weak laugh. "Like I have a clue about any of this. Anyway, Sophie should be fine in her carrier. Mom gave her a bottle before we came over, so I'm hoping she'll sleep through dinner."

Joella couldn't think of a reply, so she simply smiled and started for the kitchen.

"Anything I can do to help?" Samuel asked, following her.

"No, thanks. Go join your family. I'll just, um…"

She glanced around for something—anything—she could occupy herself with. *Get ahold of yourself, girl. You are being a ninny.*

Samuel breathed out a quiet sigh. "Look, I know you must have a lot of questions."

She forced a dismissive laugh. "Really, you don't owe me any details."

"Maybe not, but since I'll be around for a while, I'd like to hope we can still be friends."

Friends? How could he assume she'd even want to be friends after…after *everything*? "I'd rather keep things professional, if it's all the same. You have your life, and I have mine, so I think it would be best if we didn't—"

Holly bustled into the kitchen. "Excuse the interruption." Offering a sheepish grin, she edged around them to the refrigerator. "Just grabbing the bruschetta tray."

The cheesy-tomato aroma of Holly's lasagna in the oven penetrated Joella's senses. Time to put an end to this conversation that was going nowhere and return to full hostess mode. Seeing the ice bucket on the table, she snatched it. "Right behind you, Holly. Does everyone have something to drink?"

Chapter Two

After church on Sunday, Samuel welcomed his mother's help arranging Sophie's nursery. The room was actually an oversize storage closet across the hall from the apartment's only bedroom, and for now that worked fine. Samuel set up the mini crib he'd purchased before leaving Houston, and his mother borrowed a changing table with drawers from a church friend.

Mom had hinted more than once that Samuel could have his old room in the main house and they'd convert one of the guest rooms into a nursery, but Samuel declined. For one thing, he was used to his own space. But more importantly, he needed to establish a home for himself and Sophie so she'd know he was her father and that he'd always be there for her.

First thing Monday morning, though, he reluctantly deposited his baby girl in her grandmother's arms before pushing his father in his wheelchair out to the barn office.

Taking care with his casted leg and sore rib, Dad used crutches to get himself through the office door and into the chair behind the desk. With a grunt of pain, he motioned toward another chair. "Pull it around and have a seat. We'll start by going over the accounting and inventory systems."

Considering Samuel felt much more comfortable working with numbers than with horses, this was the one part of ranch work he felt even moderately qualified for. He scooted closer for a better view of the computer screen.

After barely an hour of explaining the basics, Dad grimaced and reached for his crutches. "You'll have to take it from here. I'll be in the house if you run into problems."

Samuel helped his father to his feet, then out the door and down the two steps to where he'd parked the wheelchair. "Can you make it okay?"

With a mutter that could well have been an uncharacteristic swear word, Dad squeezed his eyes shut. "I'm hurting pretty bad. If you could push me to the back porch..."

"Sure, Dad." To ask for help from anyone,

especially Samuel, the stubborn man had to be in a lot of pain.

Returning to the office a few minutes later, he frowned at the tall stack of invoices, inventory lists and employee time sheets his father had shoved in front of him. The data entry wasn't complicated, but he could clearly see why this had always been Dad's and Spencer's least favorite part of operating a quarter-horse ranch.

Sorting through the paperwork and keying numbers into the computer, he soon fell into a rhythm. By noon he'd whittled the stack down to a couple of bills with figures that didn't match with inventory. Dad should take a closer look before he wrote checks to the suppliers for items he hadn't received.

He should also look into investing in software upgrades, not to mention a new computer system. It appeared the ranch had been limping along with the same ancient computer and old-school record-keeping methods for at least ten years. Probably not a good idea to mention all this on Samuel's first day on the job, though. Dad wasn't a guy who enjoyed being blindsided, and a broken leg plus learning less than two days ago that he'd suddenly become a grandfather was probably the most he could handle for now.

Samuel massaged his forehead. He doubted his father had so much as looked at Sophie for more than a few seconds, much less held her. And he'd made no attempt at all to hide his shame and disappointment over his rebellious son's latest moral failure. What would it take to prove to his father—and everyone else who doubted him—that he'd changed?

After locking up the office, he headed to the house, anxious to see how Sophie had fared. He found his mother humming softly as she waltzed around the kitchen with Sophie snuggled against her in a scarf-like sling.

"Shh, don't wake her," Mom whispered, still swaying. "She just had her bottle and I'm getting her to sleep."

"And already spoiling her rotten. Where'd you get that sling?"

"I made it when you and Spencer were babies. Always hoped I'd get to use some of your things again with my grandbaby."

The way Mom had taken to Sophie from the start was a relief and a true blessing. Samuel could only hope Dad would eventually come to love her, too. He tiptoed closer to skim his knuckles across the sleeping baby's cheek. Sophie rewarded him with a pucker of her rosebud lips and a gentle sigh.

Dear God, I already love this baby so much! Please help me be a good dad.

"Why don't you fix some sandwiches while I put her in the bassinet." Another relic from his babyhood, no doubt. Mom started for the living room. "Everything's in the fridge."

Samuel's brows shot up. "Hang on. Why don't *I* put her down and *you* make the sandwiches?"

"Because handing her off to you will jostle her too much." She shooed him away. "You do remember how to slap ham and cheese on bread, don't you?"

Maybe having his mother babysit Sophie wasn't such a good idea after all. He'd moved in at the ranch barely forty-eight hours ago, but it felt like Mom had held his baby more than he had, at least during the day. He'd never admit how he spent most nights dozing in the old upholstered rocking recliner with Sophie tucked like a bowlegged little frog upon his chest. He could never get enough of the lavender scent of baby shampoo and the cottony feel of her downy-soft sleeper. And wasn't there something about bonding with a baby through the sound of your heartbeat?

While Samuel scraped mustard and mayo across bread slices, his grandfather ambled into the kitchen. *"¿Dónde está la niña?"* he asked—*Where is the baby?* "I haven't had a chance to hold her yet today. Your mother is so selfish, Enrique."

"Tell me about it," Samuel muttered. He let it slide that Tito—short for the Spanish *abuelito*, "grandfather"—had called him by Dad's given name. "Mom's putting her down for a nap."

Typically grouchy and aloof, Tito had smiled more the past couple of days than Samuel could remember in his entire lifetime. The attention the old man showered on his great-granddaughter almost made up for Samuel's father's utter lack of interest.

Mom returned, pushing Dad to the table in his wheelchair. After Dad offered a curt blessing, Mom asked, "How'd it go in the office this morning?"

"Fine," Samuel said. "I think I'm catching on."

Dad helped himself to some potato chips, then passed the bag to Samuel. "Did you get through those invoices?"

"There are a couple I need to ask you about."

"Can it wait?" With a subtle nod toward Tito, Mom said, "I need to borrow Samuel this afternoon for that *thing* we talked about. It shouldn't take more than an hour or so."

Thing? What was his mother setting him up for now?

"Go ahead," Dad said with a shrug. "Spencer is coming over to review the training schedule."

Mom studied him, concern narrowing her eyes. "Are you sure you're not overdoing it? The doctor said you should be getting plenty of rest while you heal."

"Don't coddle me." Jaw clenched, Dad drummed a fist on the table. He glared at Samuel. "One baby in this house is more than enough."

"Hank, please." Mom cast Dad a chiding frown. "Yes, you definitely need a nice, long nap *and* an attitude adjustment."

They finished lunch in strained silence. Afterward, Mom instructed Samuel to pack up the diaper bag while she nestled Sophie in the sling.

Samuel trailed his mother out the back door. "Hey, want to tell me where we're going?"

Once they were outside, she told him they were meeting with Joella about Tito's party. "I thought we'd walk rather than fuss with trying to get Sophie buckled into the car seat. I need to talk to you about a couple of things on the way."

Samuel wasn't sure why he was needed at a discussion about his grandfather's surprise birthday party, but after spending the morning cooped up in the barn office, he couldn't refuse the chance to stretch his legs and breathe fresh air. They took the long way around, walking down the lane to the road. "What did you need to talk to me about?"

Mom's steps slowed. "Honey, you know I love you, and I'm over-the-moon thrilled to have a granddaughter." She didn't have to speak the implied *even under the circumstances*. "But as much as I enjoy spending time with Sophie, I can't be your full-time babysitter."

Heat rushed up Samuel's neck. "I never intended to take advantage. But I'm so far out of my depth here—learning how to take care of a baby, and now trying to get up to speed with managing the office."

"I know you're doing your best. And I'll still be here for you. But having to keep an eye on your grandfather as he gets older, and now with your dad laid up for several weeks, I just can't take on much more." She pulled in a breath. "If this weren't a milestone birthday for Arturo, plus the fact that we don't know how much longer we'll have him around, I'd seriously consider calling off the party."

"No, it's important," Samuel said. "If there's anything I can do to help, you know I will.

And don't worry about Sophie. I'll figure out something, I promise."

What, exactly, he had no idea. The thought of leaving his baby with strangers at a day-care center in town certainly held no appeal. Maybe he could keep her with him in the office. Except he could only imagine how distracted he'd be—not wise while attempting to work with numbers and spreadsheets.

They'd turned up the McClement driveway, past the crumbling Austin-stone bases where the arched gate to Rancho de Manos y Corazón—Hands and Heart Ranch—once stood, long before Samuel's time. The cattle ranch had been the joint endeavor of Samuel's grandfather and the late Egan McClement, army buddies who'd served together in the Korean War. No one knew what had ultimately come between the friends, but around fifty years ago, they'd severed the friendship and divided the ranch with that ugly stretch of barbed wire. The McClements had continued with cattle ranching, while Arturo Navarro, with his *charro* heritage—Mexican horsemanship—turned his attention to raising and training quarter horses.

Lindsey's aunt Audra greeted them at the front door, then showed them to the study, where Joella and Holly were waiting. "Lindsey and I will help with the party arrangements as needed," Audra explained, "but…considering everything…we both think it best if we keep a low profile."

Would the day ever come when the decades-old Navarro-McClement feud no longer cast its shadow on the present? Samuel could only pray that Tito would find it in his heart to mend fences—both figuratively and literally—before he died.

Pulling up chairs for them at the worktable, Holly Elliot beamed at the sleeping baby. "Is she always so good?"

"Pretty much." Samuel's mother eased into one of the chairs. "I can hardly take my eyes off this sweet thing."

Joella kept her distance but tilted her head with a wistful smile. "She's a beautiful baby."

In the next instant, her smile chilled. She straightened and cleared her throat. "So let's talk about the party. I made a few calls this morning and may have a lead on the entertainment."

The change in Joella had been so abrupt that Samuel suffered a moment of mental whiplash. While his mother and Joella discussed bands and music styles, he contemplated the woman across from him. He hadn't forgotten her coolness toward him Saturday evening.

Was she judging him for what he'd let happen with Chelsea…or for what he'd let happen fourteen years ago in the barn loft?

"It would help if we could see the building where the celebration will be held," Joella was saying. "Once I can visualize what we have to work with, it'll be easier to plan the layout."

"Samuel can give you a tour this afternoon," his mother said. Sophie began to squirm and whimper, and Mom rocked her gently. "Actually, Samuel, would you mind running point with Joella on the party arrangements?"

"What—me?" Samuel jerked forward. "Mom, I know I said I'd help, but this isn't exactly what I had in mind."

"You won't have to do much, just coordinate with whatever Joella needs. And you can always ask me if anything comes up that you can't handle."

Like taking care of my baby and learning the ranch business while planning a party with a woman who clearly wants nothing to do with me?

"It's almost feeding time again," his mother said, rising. "I should take this sweetie home. Samuel, you can come for her as soon as you finish with Joella. Your dad and I decided the old white barn with the green trim will work best."

Samuel helped his mother to her feet. "I can take Sophie now. Shouldn't you stay and finish whatever you came over to talk about?"

"No, I've covered everything I needed to for now. Besides, I've left your dad on his own long enough. Just drop the diaper bag at the house on your way over with Joella." With Sophie's whimpers edging toward a full-blown hunger cry, Mom said a quick goodbye and hurried out.

Holly sighed as she watched them leave. "This is bringing back memories of when Davey was a baby. I miss those days."

Joella leaned sideways to give her friend a hug. Samuel's mother had told him Holly's husband had died in an accident a few years ago, and now she was raising a son with a seizure disorder. Hard enough being a single parent, as he was learning. He couldn't imagine Holly's struggles. *Dear God, please keep my little girl safe and healthy.*

Joella's tender show of concern for Holly touched something deep within Samuel, but there was also something else in her expression, and it seemed almost like...longing. Whatever it was, she quickly recovered by shoving her notebook and cell phone into a tote. "Shall we get going? I don't want to take up too much of your time."

"Snap lots of photos," Holly said, gathering her things.

Joella looked momentarily unsettled. "You're not coming with us?"

"Can't. It's almost time to pick up Davey from school. Text me the pictures later."

Blinking as Holly left, Joella turned to Samuel. "I guess it's just you and me, then."

"If you'd rather wait..."

"No time like the present." Her jaunty laugh didn't match the hesitation in her eyes. She motioned toward the door.

Hefting the diaper bag, Samuel glanced toward the hallway, then back at Joella. "If this is making you uncomfortable, just say the word and I'll tell Mom I need to bow out."

"Don't bother." Her chin lifted. "I prefer to honor my commitments."

Did he sense condemnation in her tone? No use trying to defend himself when she'd already made up her mind about him. Wishing her opinion didn't matter so much, he released a quiet sigh. "All right, then. Let's go see the barn."

Before walking next door with Samuel, Joella went upstairs to get a sweater. She'd dressed in a comfy pair of jeans that morning but decided to change from her casual flats into a sturdy pair of sneakers. No telling what she might encounter in a horse barn, not to mention how much work lay ahead to get the barn clean enough for a festive birthday gala.

Guess she was about to find out.

Stepping onto the front porch with her, Samuel asked, "Shortcut through the pasture, or shall we take the road?"

"Pasture's fine." She pointed to her jeans and sneakers. "I believe I'm dressed appropriately."

He shrugged. "Shortcut it is."

As they neared the gap in the barbed-wire fence, Joella slowed her steps as teenage memories returned. How many times that long-ago summer had she and Lindsey sneaked between the separated strands of barbed wire so they could hang out with Samuel and Spencer? The boys had chosen the partially concealed location to keep their grumpy old grandfather from realizing they'd invited a McClement and her friend onto Navarro land.

Samuel ducked through the opening first, then took Joella's hand to steady her as she slipped between the wires. It was all she could do not to react to his touch, and she withdrew her hand the instant she could do so gracefully.

They came out next to one of the smaller

barns. "We'll cut around back and over to the old barn Mom was talking about. And watch your step," he warned as they crossed one of the horse paddocks. "It's a manure minefield."

A reddish-brown horse with a white blaze down its face gave a curious nicker and wandered closer. Joella instinctively edged closer to Samuel. "Should we be worried?"

"Not a bit. That's Loretta, one of our old broodmares. She's enjoying retirement now." Samuel led them out the gate on the opposite side of the paddock. "Wait here while I run the diaper bag in the house."

While Samuel headed inside, Joella rested her arms on the fence rail and used the time alone to regain her equilibrium. Why did being near Samuel still have to affect her so? It wasn't as if there could ever be anything between them...for so many reasons.

Loretta sauntered over and offered her chin for a scratch. "I remember you now," she told the mare. "I think I even rode you once or twice back in the day. You always took real good care of me."

Lips pinched, she reminded herself not to get too confident about being able to dredge up fifteen-year-old memories. More critical was what she could remember from ten minutes ago, or yesterday, or last month. No one, not even her best friends, knew she lived in constant dread of developing the early-onset Alzheimer's that had stolen her mother from her day by devastating day.

And being around Samuel wasn't helping. The impulsive, freewheeling teenage boy she'd once found so beguiling had matured into an incredibly handsome adult—a man she could easily lose her heart to all over again if she weren't keeping it locked down tight.

Best to keep reminding herself he'd fathered a child with someone else, with apparently no intention of marrying the baby's mother. Saturday night after everyone else had gone, Lindsey had finished telling Joella about the letter Sophie's mother had left for Samuel. Even if her reasons for giving the baby to him were valid, how could he simply walk away from the mother of his child? So much for honor and responsibility.

She glanced over her shoulder to see him jogging her way and hoped her expression wouldn't give away her thoughts. "Everything okay with Sophie?"

"Sleeping peacefully, for now." Frowning, he shot a quick glance toward the house. "Afraid I can't take too long at the barn. I need to get back before she wakes up so I can relieve Mom."

"Is there a problem?" It was only polite to ask.

"We're still working a few things out about baby care." As they started walking, he muttered, "I don't know why Chelsea ever thought I could do this."

Chelsea—Sophie's mother. The spoken name set an odious brew of emotions churning in Joella's abdomen. Before she could stop herself, she burst out, "Then maybe you should have done the right thing and married her."

Samuel stopped short, his face contorted as he glared at her. "You don't think I would have, if that's what she wanted? Don't pass judgment when you don't know the whole story." With a brisk shake of his head, he marched away.

"Samuel, wait." Regret choking her, Joella hurried to catch up. "My remark was completely out of line. Your situation is none of my business and I'm sorry."

He slowed his steps but kept his gaze straight ahead. "And I apologize for snapping back. I'm just..." His shoulders heaved with a long, pained breath. "I'm doing the best I can here. *Nothing* about the past week has gone anything like I'd imagined."

"No, I suppose not." Empathy crept in,

crowding out her unjustified resentment. Her mother's Alzheimer's, losing her father only months after her mother died, then the devastating mistake that cost her her job—oh, yes, she knew plenty about having her world turned inside out by the unexpected.

"If it makes any difference in your opinion of me," he began with a sigh, "understand that I'd never close the door on Sophie's mother. If she ever changes her mind about being in Sophie's life, the attorney knows where to find me."

"I… I suppose that's all you can do, then. I can see how much you love your baby girl, and love is what matters most." She cleared her throat to disguise the telltale crack in her voice. She needed to work harder at keeping things professional between them before she opened herself up to all kinds of trouble.

"Thank you. For that much, at least." He pointed past the main barn and training arena. "We should keep going. The barn's this way."

They followed a narrow lane to a smaller, older-looking barn. The wooden structure looked well-kept and had been recently painted, with white walls and pine-green trim. A cupola and weather vane perched on the crest of the roof. This was a section of the ranch Joella recalled as being off-limits when they were kids.

"Navarro Quarter Horses started right here," Samuel said as he slid open the tall entrance doors. A subtle but clear note of deference had replaced the acrimony in his tone. "My grandfather and Egan McClement built this barn together."

"Lindsey's grandfather." Joella's words echoed in the cavernous space. "Before the feud started, obviously."

"They were partners in everything at first. No one besides Tito seems to know exactly what went wrong, and he won't talk about it."

"Lindsey has told me her grandparents kept it to themselves, too. Whatever happened must have caused a lot of pain on both sides." She stepped farther inside, not a little surprised at how tidy everything was. "Are you sure it's a good idea to celebrate your grandfather's birthday in the barn a McClement helped to build?"

"As the beginnings of the Navarro ranching legacy, this place has always meant a lot to him." Samuel's mouth hardened. "I'm sure by now he's blocked Egan's involvement from memory."

Time to change the subject. Joella walked over to peer into one of the stalls. "Everything looks so clean and neat. Does this barn even get used anymore?"

"Not often. Ever since Dad and Tito added

the bigger, more modern barns, it's mainly been used for overflow or the occasional boarder, like when clients leave their horse for extended training."

Turning slowly, Joella cast an appraising eye across the wide central space beneath the vaulted roof. She could picture a stage for the band at the far end, with tables and chairs grouped around the dance floor. The stalls along the side walls would be perfect for food and beverage stations. Pulling out her phone, she nodded appreciatively and started snapping photos. "We can definitely make this work."

"Great. So what's next?" He didn't sound the least bit enthusiastic. More like he only wanted to get this over with.

She tried not to take it personally, although he likely meant it that way. She stowed her phone and tugged out her organizer notebook. "Now the real planning begins. Seating arrangements, menu selections, decorations, musicians—"

Releasing an uneasy chuckle, Samuel lifted both hands. "You're the expert. Unless there's something else you need from me right now, I should go get Sophie."

"If you'd encourage your parents to firm up the guest list, I'd appreciate it. In my business, everything's about numbers, so I need an approximate head count ASAP."

"I'll remind them."

"Thanks. I know you have other things to do, and so do I." Tucking her notebook away, she turned to go.

"Can you find your way back?"

"Yes, I think so, if you'll point me in—" The ringing of Samuel's cell phone interrupted her.

He glanced at it. "It's my mom. Hang on a sec." Stepping to one side, he answered the call. "Hi, Mom. We're just leaving the barn. Joella says it'll work fine, but she needs a head count soon… Sure, we'll be right there."

"Everything okay?" Joella asked as he ended the call.

"Tito's napping, so Mom asked if you could come by the house. She had a couple more thoughts about the party arrangements."

She nodded, and a few minutes later he showed her in through the kitchen door.

"We're in the living room," Lois called in a soft, chirpy voice. "Sophie's awake. Come say hi."

Samuel's whole body pitched slightly forward like a sprinter at the starting line. He looked as if he'd quite forgotten Joella's presence. Following him into the room, she glimpsed Lois seated in a glider-style rocker with matching footstool. The woman hummed a lilting melody as the baby gazed up at her from the cradle of her arms. Joella had kept her distance Saturday evening during Spencer and Lindsey's welcome-home dinner, and after only a brief glimpse this afternoon, she'd seen little more than a wisp of Sophie's brown hair from within the sling Lois had carried her in.

Now, for the first time, she had an up-close, unhindered view of the sweet face, with those curious gray eyes and a tiny, heart-shaped mouth as pink as a perfect little rose.

"Oh," she whispered, her throat clenching. Unable to resist, she leaned closer to touch the baby's plump, velvety-soft cheek. "Oh, she's precious."

"Want to hold her?" Lois offered.

"I, uh..." She forced a painful swallow. "I don't have much experience with babies."

"Nothing to it. Here, Samuel, hold Sophie for a sec while I trade places with Joella." Lois gently passed the baby to Samuel and then rose from the glider.

Not at all sure how it happened, Joella found herself in the chair. Her pulse hammered.

Samuel stood over her, a doubtful look on his face. "Ready?"

"What do I do?"

"The main thing is to support her head."

Slowly, he lowered Sophie into her arms. “There, like that.”

Watching from the sofa, Lois gave a soft laugh. “She won’t break, honey. It’s okay to breathe.”

Realizing she *had* been holding her breath, she glanced up to find Samuel’s gaze locked with hers. The frown had eased, and now a crooked grin skewed his lips. “See?” he said. “Not so hard, is it?”

With a slow, deliberate exhalation, she looked down at the baby, who’d drawn her tiny caterpillar brows together in a studious expression.

“Hello, little one,” Joella murmured. The most amazing sense of delight swelled beneath her heart, and tears pricked the backs of her eyelids. She sniffed and swallowed in a futile effort to hold them back. Swiping at the escaping wetness, she lifted the baby toward Samuel. “Take her, please. I… I need to go.”

Samuel scooped up the baby. “Joella—”

She waved him off as she pushed to her feet. “Sorry, we’ll talk more about the party later, okay?”

Before either Samuel or Lois could stop her, she rushed out the front door. By the time she reached the road, her face was awash in tears, and her heart felt as if it could shatter. Until the moment Samuel had placed Sophie in her arms, she'd been able to keep the longing for a family of her own locked away. But once she'd felt the baby's warm little body against her chest, once she'd been captured and held by those wide and shimmering gray eyes, all hope of maintaining her facade of serene detachment had been lost.

Chapter Three

For the rest of the day, Samuel couldn't shake the memory of Joella's stricken face when she'd thrust Sophie into his arms and made a mad dash for the door.

Later that evening, Mom called Joella to make sure she was okay. "She claims it was nothing," she told Samuel afterward. "An unexpected emotional reaction, she said, and she hurried out because she was embarrassed."

To Samuel, it had sure seemed like a lot more than embarrassment over getting choked up, and he suspected his mother hadn't been totally convinced, either. Was it something about the baby? Was she still judging him because he hadn't made the effort to track down Chelsea and marry her?

In the meantime, he had other matters to worry about, number one being how to manage

Sophie's care during the day without his mother's help. He couldn't ignore the fatigue etching Mom's face these days, much less blame her for being unable to take on nanny duties on top of nursing Dad back to health, dealing with Tito's mercurial moods and now arranging for the big birthday bash.

Over the next few days, his mother continued caring for Sophie in the mornings. After lunch, Samuel brought her to the barn office with him and tried to get a little work done while she napped in her infant seat between feedings and diaper changes. It was far from an ideal situation, though, since every time the phone rang, she'd startle awake and then cry until he either picked her up or bounced her infant seat with his foot while he dealt with the caller.

On Saturday afternoon, between rocking Sophie and shuffling employee work schedules for the upcoming week, he almost didn't hear the office door click open. Spencer's greeting surprised him.

"Still at it?" his twin asked as he sauntered into the room. His dusty hat and jeans suggested he'd just finished another horse training session. "It's only your first week on the job. Do I need to ask Dad to go easier on you?"

Groaning, Samuel pushed aside the computer keyboard and tilted back in his chair, Sophie nestled against his chest. "I'm still at it *because* it's only my first week on the job. And it's all your fault, by the way, leaving files in such a mess."

"Desk work was never my thing."

"Just like horses were never mine."

"Hey, Slam, I didn't mean anything—"

"No, Spiny, it's me." It was both funny and touching how their childhood nicknames for each other had resurfaced lately. He gave his right eye socket a one-finger massage. "It's been a long week, that's all. Since Dad set me loose in here, I've tried not to bother him any more than necessary. Then Mom made me the go-to person for Tito's birthday party that he's not supposed to know about. Plus I'm doing all this while figuring out how to survive as a single dad."

Spencer sank into one of the visitor chairs. "Wow, I'm sorry, man. Is there anything I can do to help?"

"I wouldn't say no to free babysitting."

"Childcare is *really* not my thing. I could talk to Lindsey, except she and Audra are getting ready for those bred heifers to calve, so she's already dividing her time between the cattle and River Bend Events." Lips pursed,

Spencer scratched his chin. "Have you thought of asking Joella?"

Samuel grimaced. "I don't think she's comfortable around babies. Besides, have you noticed I'm not exactly her favorite person?"

"I seem to recall all kinds of sparks flying between you two that summer when we were teens. What happened?"

He was pretty sure his brother knew nothing of the night he'd spent with Joella in the barn loft. But Spencer was well aware of how far Samuel had drifted from God as an adult. Hard to miss when a major piece of evidence snuggled right here on Samuel's chest. He gave his brother a look that said as much.

"Well, you're both adults now, and given time, I'm sure Joella will come to see you've put your old life behind you. Besides, if Lindsey can forgive me for how I snubbed her when we were kids, there's definitely hope for you and Joella."

"This isn't quite the same thing, but I appreciate the vote of confidence." Sophie had fallen back asleep, so Samuel laid her in the infant seat and then scooted up to the desk. "If you really want to make yourself useful, bring a chair around and help me sort out these work assignments."

Spencer was much more familiar with the

staff, so it didn't take long to finish filling in next week's schedule. After shutting things down, they took Sophie to the house. Not long afterward, Tito appeared, demanding to hold the baby. Samuel never tired of seeing his grandfather show so much joy and affection for his great-granddaughter. It was a shame Dad was still avoiding her. Did he even realize what he was missing out on?

Knowing he'd have Sophie to himself tonight, Samuel left his brother and grandfather making silly sounds and generally acting goofy over a baby who was still too young to appreciate their antics. He'd relish a quick nap but instead grabbed a light jacket and went outside for some fresh air.

Sounds of music and laughter drifted across the field between the ranches. With the sun slipping behind the hills, the strings of miniature lights in the backyard next door twinkled like fireflies. Was it only two weeks ago the McClement house and chapel had been similarly decorated for Spencer's wedding? Hard to believe how much his life had changed since then.

Best he could tell from this side of the barbed-wire fence, it looked like an older crowd. Then Joella stepped off the back porch, and a sudden ache throbbed behind his sternum. He took a giant step backward, as if another two feet separating him and Joella would be enough to slow his racing heart. This wasn't attraction—*couldn't* be. For one reason, he was supremely committed to getting a handle on fatherhood. For another, Joella had been projecting major keep-your-distance vibes, not the least concerning of which was how she'd rushed off the other day after holding Sophie.

And Spencer seriously thought she'd be open to helping with Sophie's care? Not at all likely.

Across the way, Joella spoke a few words to Holly and Lindsey, then returned to the back porch and surveyed the yard briefly before going back inside. Moments later, a motion at the front of the house drew Samuel's attention. One hand clutching her stomach, Joella paced along the circle driveway, her distress obvious.

His inner debate raged for about half a minute—pretend he hadn't seen her and slink back inside, or get his sorry self over there and ask how he could help?

Concern won out. He vaulted over the barbed-wire fence and jogged across the field. As he rounded the house, Joella jerked her head up in surprise.

"Sorry, didn't mean to startle you." Slowing, he held one hand out toward her. "I was watching you and—" Great, now he sounded like a stalker. "I mean, I came outside for air and could see you looked upset. Is everything okay?"

"I'm fine." Clearly not, judging from the angry set of her jaw. Her attempt at a smile lasted less than a nanosecond. "Okay, I'm *not* fine. This was supposed to be a couple's renewal of wedding vows, and the officiant is going to be late."

An inconvenience, yes, but earth-shattering enough to warrant Joella's extreme reaction? Samuel scratched the nape of his neck. "What happened—car trouble?"

"I wish. He's saying I told him seven thirty, but the Hoffmans were expecting him at six, and that's the time I have down in my planner." She started pacing again. "I'm certain I told him six o'clock when I made the arrangements."

He strode over, halting her with a gentle grip on her shoulders. "Come on. It can't be that bad." When he tried to meet her gaze, she kept her eyes averted. "It sounds like a simple misunderstanding. From what I could tell, the guests out back are happily mingling and munching on whatever food Holly's serving up."

"I know, I know. I'm overreacting." She

clamped a palm against her forehead. "But I can't afford one more mistake—"

"Wait. How are *you* at fault if you told him the right time? He probably wrote it down wrong."

"Or maybe I'm the one who got mixed up. I mean, it wouldn't be—" She cut herself off abruptly and spun out of his grasp.

"Take a breath, Joella." He'd tried for a soothing tone, but he couldn't hide his growing confusion. She had to be blowing the whole thing out of proportion. He checked his watch—barely six fifteen. "If he's coming from Gabriel Bend, he won't be that late. Is he on his way?"

Exhaling through pursed lips, she gave a harsh nod. "I think so." Facing him directly, she squared her shoulders. This time, her smile held a bit more assurance. "I'm pulling myself together now. Can you pretend you didn't see any of this?"

He could lie and say yes, but it wouldn't be so easy to forget the vulnerability he'd witnessed, not just this evening but the other day with Sophie as well.

Before he could reply, a compact blue sedan roared up the drive, pulling up behind Joella. Samuel grabbed her elbow in case he had to yank her out of harm's way, but the driver braked in the nick of time.

A frazzled-looking man in a black suit and clerical collar heaved his bulk from behind the wheel. Huffing and puffing, he stumbled toward them. "Ms. James, please forgive me. After you called, I double-checked my datebook, and there it was—six o'clock, just as you said. I'd mentally confused this event with the Bible class I'm leading tomorrow."

"Well, you're here now." The consummate professional once more, Joella slipped her arm through the minister's. "Let me show you to the chapel and we can get started."

The minister might be oblivious to the visible relief coursing through Joella, but Samuel had noticed. He suspected it had less to do with the man's arrival and more because his tardiness had admittedly been his error and not hers.

And what had she meant by *one more mistake*?

By Monday morning, Joella had almost gotten over Saturday's humiliating meltdown.

Almost.

Because why did Samuel have to be looking her way at the exact moment she'd lost her cool—and less than a week after she'd practically thrown his baby at him and rushed out of the Navarros' house in tears? She had to work with him for the next few weeks, and they were already walking on eggshells around each other. Now he must think her a fragile female who fell apart at the slightest provocation.

This time, anyway, the error hadn't been hers, and even if it had been, no lives were at risk. As long as she lived, she'd never forget the feeling of utter helplessness—and unrelenting guilt—as a client's toddler experienced a severe allergic reaction to something the caterer had served containing peanuts. If not for quick use of an EpiPen, the child could have died.

Perhaps she would forget…someday…

For now, though, she intended to get back into the fitness routine she'd been neglecting. And not just aerobic exercise, but a wholesome diet, stress reduction and all the other aspects of healthy living she'd recently let go by the wayside.

Dressed in a sweatshirt, leggings and running shoes, she secured her hair in a ponytail beneath a baseball cap. Downstairs in the kitchen, she poured herself half a mug of coffee. She could always count on Audra to set a pot to brew before starting early-morning ranch chores.

While she sipped, Spencer came in the back door. Brows shooting skyward, he tossed his Stetson onto a hook. "You're up earlier than usual."

"Thought I'd go running, if my legs can remember how." She smirked. "I don't suppose there's much chance of convincing Lindsey to join me."

Chuckling, Spencer slipped out of his Sherpa-lined jacket. "Pretty sure running is not Lindsey's thing. Least of all at six thirty in the morning."

"Figured. If she's up before I'm back, tell her I won't be long." After rinsing her mug in the sink, Joella headed outside.

The chill in the early-March air made her suck in a breath. She jogged down the back porch steps, then down the driveway. It was still fairly dark, but her sweatshirt was pale pink and her shoes had reflectors, so she should be visible enough. Besides, they rarely had much traffic out this way any time of day.

When she turned onto the road, the last thing she expected was to run—literally—into Samuel Navarro.

"Whoa, whoa!" He braced her before they both toppled over. "Sorry, you came out of nowhere."

"I came out of my own driveway," she said,

panting. How could she already be out of breath? "Besides, you're wearing practically all black. Don't you know better?"

"My bad. I was only thinking about getting in a quick run before Sophie wakes up to be fed."

"You left her *alone*?"

"No, she's with Mom." He sounded hurt that she'd even suggest such a thing.

Her turn to apologize. "I should have realized. Sorry. And sorry for interrupting your run. Excuse me. I'll just—"

"No problem. Anyway, looks like we were going the same direction...if you don't mind running together." Those big brown eyes that had made her knees go weak as a sixteen-year-old had pretty much the same effect now.

Which made his suggestion *so* not a good idea. "I'm kind of out of shape. Wouldn't want to hold you back."

"Doubt I'll make it very far myself. How about we take it easy, for both our sakes?" Tipping his head in a signal for her to come along, he started up the road.

Now it would be rude to refuse. Their footfalls synchronized as she fell in step beside him, and for several minutes they jogged without speaking...until her compulsion to say something about Saturday evening grew too strong.

"That thing the other night," she began, the slap of her sneakers punctuating her words. "River Bend Events is just getting off the ground, and we can't afford any negative PR. Obviously, I didn't handle the mix-up very well."

Samuel didn't reply right away. Listening to his huffing breaths, she could only wonder what he was thinking. He cast her a quick glance. "I admit I've been concerned. Feeling better about things now?"

The question had no easy answer. "I'm working on it."

The sky had lightened slightly, revealing the scraggly shapes of mesquite and cedar trees bordering the road. Beyond the fence line, prickly-pear cacti dotted pastureland where cows or horses grazed. The crisp air carried an earthy freshness, so different from big-city suburbia. This *had* to be a healthy change of pace.

Approaching a crossroads, they slowed. That was fine with Joella, because she was getting a stitch in her side. Halting at the stop sign, she pressed a hand against her ribs. "Keep going if you want to. I've about reached my limit."

"Same here. This is far enough for me."

Sweat dripping from his brow, Samuel bent forward, bracing his hands on his thighs. "Told you I hadn't done this in a while. How about we walk back?"

She nodded with relief, and they turned toward home. "Guess we should both be doing this more often."

"I do a lot better when I have a running partner to keep me accountable." Samuel cast a hesitant glance her way. "That is, if you're interested."

"I don't know. I mean, I'm not sure how consistent I can be."

He snickered. "Consistency is the whole reason for having an accountability partner."

She couldn't argue. And where else would she find one out here? Lindsey obviously wouldn't get up with her at the crack of dawn to go running.

But *Samuel*?

"If you'd prefer to run alone, I totally get it. I shouldn't have asked."

"It isn't that." She massaged the slowly ebbing twinge in her side. "It's just that things between us have been…tense. Not to mention occasionally embarrassing."

"If this is still about Saturday evening, I get it. You wanted everything to be perfect for your client."

"Not just our client. Lindsey created River Bend Events because she and Audra need the extra income to keep the McClement ranch afloat. And Holly uprooted herself and her son to move to Gabriel Bend and partner with us. They've invested so much of themselves in this venture, and I love them too much to let them down."

Samuel's brow furrowed. "But you've sacrificed a lot, too, giving up your career in Dallas to come here. How could the success of this partnership be all on you?"

"Because—" She clamped her lips together. The reasons were too complicated to explain. Although, in some ways, it was a relief he'd jumped on Saturday's meltdown instead of how she'd humiliated herself the day he'd let her hold his baby.

After a brief silence, he said, "Well, I don't think you're giving yourself enough credit. You're obviously very skilled at what you do."

She tilted her head to cast him a surprised but grateful smile. "That's kind of you to say."

"I, on the other hand..." A ragged breath escaped Samuel's chest. "What have I gotten myself into?"

If you haven't figured it out by now, she wanted to say. But his tortured expression stifled the cutting reply before it could leave her lips. Like her, he was a victim of his own mistakes, and looking backward didn't make those mistakes go away. "Maybe you're not giving yourself enough credit, either," she began slowly. "It's clear you're striving hard to be both a good son and a good father. It can't be easy."

They'd reached the McClement driveway, where he paused to face her. "And that's very kind of *you* to say. Really, Joella. Thank you."

"Don't thank me for speaking the truth. I'm sorry I haven't shown more understanding for how difficult your situation is."

"Thanks. So… I don't suppose there's any chance you'd reconsider letting us be friends?"

His charming smile and puppy-dog eyes threatened to turn her knees to rubber—which wouldn't take much after her first run/walk in forever. But she couldn't give in. "As I told you before, I'd rather keep things professional between us, all things considered."

All things considered? Obviously, she still held his moral failures against him. "Sure, if that's what you want." He checked the time on his Fitbit. "I want to spend some time with Sophie before I have to get to work. Thanks for the run."

Without looking back, he picked up his pace

and sprinted home. This day had definitely not started out as expected.

Upstairs in the apartment, he changed into jeans and a long-sleeved polo. After downing a bowl of cereal, he went to the house for a few minutes with his baby girl. While he gave her a bottle as they rocked in the glider, he mentally reviewed the work awaiting him in the barn office. Could he plow through the most pressing items this morning before he took over Sophie's care after lunch?

The creak of his father's wheelchair sounded in the hallway—they'd rented a hospital bed for him and set it up in the den—and shortly Dad rolled himself into the living room. "You'll need to drive over to Austin later."

This was news. "Why?"

"To pick up the portable steel corral panels I had on order. They were supposed to come in over the weekend." With a muffled groan, Dad shifted in the chair.

"Are you okay?"

"Hurting a bit. Hard to—" A cough interrupted Dad's words, and the grimace that followed left no doubt as to the severity of his pain.

"Take it easy. I'll get Mom." With Sophie tucked against his chest, Samuel pushed up from the glider.

"No, she has enough to worry about." Fist to his mouth to stifle another cough, Dad shook his head. "Go on to the office. The information about the corral panels should be in the orange desk tray."

No use arguing—Dad had definitely inherited his stubborn streak from Tito. It also wasn't lost on Samuel that, yet again, his father hadn't so much as acknowledged Sophie. "It's okay, sweetheart," he murmured against his baby's downy cap of dark hair. "Your grandpa's heart is softer than he wants anyone to know. He'll warm up to you one of these days."

He found his mother in the laundry room starting a batch of clothes, and despite his father's instructions to the contrary, he told her about Dad's coughing and obvious discomfort.

She skewed her lips. "He had a really bad night. I'll keep an eye on him."

"I could try to keep Sophie with me today, except Dad's sending me to Austin to pick up some stuff." As he patted the baby's back, she erupted in a loud, formula-scented burp. He and his mother both laughed.

Mom closed the lid and started the washer. With a smile that barely masked her fatigue, she reached for Sophie. "We'll manage, hon.

You handle whatever your dad needs you to do. That's the best way to stop him from fretting."

"If you say so." Samuel had his doubts, and he worried about his mother, too, but he dropped a kiss on Sophie's forehead and strode out to the barn.

He found the printout for the corral panels in the desk tray and copied the company's address into his phone so he'd have the directions later, then set to work entering last week's time sheet reports into the ancient computer. When it froze up for the third time that morning, he did another reboot. While he waited for the system to restart, an idea occurred to him.

After some searching with his phone browser, he chose one of the larger breeding and training facilities in the Austin area and placed a call.

"Rolling Hills Quarter Horses. AJ Bell speaking."

Samuel introduced himself. "I'm filling in as office manager for Navarro Quarter Horses, but my dad's pretty much thrown me into the deep end. Any chance I could pick your brain for an hour or so? I'll be over that way later today."

"Happy to talk. Text me when you're close and I'll meet you at the office."

It would mean leaving Sophie with Mom

longer than he probably should, but he hoped to return armed with ideas for streamlining the office work. And that would benefit all of them.

Chapter Four

At home after the run with Samuel, Joella freshened up and toasted a bagel to have with her second cup of coffee.

He only wants to be friends, she told herself. Why was she having such a hard time with the idea?

And why did her heart do the cha-cha every time she thought about seeing him again?

"Joella?" A hand waved in front of her face as she sat at the kitchen table. "Are you in there?"

Blinking several times, she looked up to see Lindsey standing over her. "Sorry, I was miles away."

"So I noticed." Lindsey quirked a brow. "Anywhere special?"

It took Joella a couple of sconds for her friend's words to sink in. She rolled her eyes.

"Just thinking about everything I need to do this week."

Lindsey filled a coffee mug, then pulled out a chair and plopped down. "Just reminding you, the cows should start calving any day now, so Audra and I will have our hands full. Which means I may not be available as much for event business."

"We should be okay." Directing her thoughts to more productive purposes, Joella did a mental review of the River Bend Events schedule. "The next thing on the docket is the mayor's daughter's sixteenth birthday party the end of the month. Holly's already heard back from them about the menu. I've booked a local DJ, and the party tent, tables and chairs will be delivered the day before."

"Sounds like you have it under control." Lindsey popped up to give Joella a quick hug. "Sometimes I have to pinch myself to believe you and Holly actually moved here to partner with me."

Joella gave her a return squeeze. "And we're loving every minute of it." *Except for one teensy complication with the initials SN.*

Lindsey settled into her chair and took a sip of coffee. "So… Arturo's party. How's that going?"

"Plans are taking shape. I need to make a few more calls later."

A disgruntled sigh slipped from Lindsey's lips. "I'm not sorry we missed Arturo's grumpy presence at our wedding, but I can tell his absence disappointed Spencer." Her gaze drifted in the direction of the Navarro ranch. "Spencer and I pray every night that Arturo will find healing for whatever issues he had with my grandfather."

"I think Lois is hoping the party will help somehow, maybe inspire him to focus on the good memories. Did you know we'll be using the original barn? They've kept it up really well—" Joella's cell phone vibrated in her jeans pocket. She shifted to retrieve it. "It's Lois, probably with more to discuss about the party."

"Go ahead. I was supposed to be helping Audra with the cows an hour ago."

While Lindsey grabbed a jacket and hurried out the back door, Joella answered the call.

"I hate to bother you," Lois began, sounding distracted, "but I need a favor. Hank's in a lot of pain this morning and having trouble breathing. I need to get him to the doctor."

"Oh, no. How can I help?"

"Samuel isn't here, and I need someone to watch Sophie. Arturo said he'd look after her, but he's been a little forgetful lately, and I'm uneasy about leaving her alone with him. For obvious reasons, I can't ask Lindsey or Audra to come over." Sounding apologetic, Lois asked, "Would you mind?"

Joella chewed her lip. This request was light-years out of her comfort zone, but Lois sounded desperate. "Okay, sure. I'm on my way."

Ten minutes later, she stood in the Navarros' kitchen doing her best to commit to memory everything Lois was telling her about feeding schedules, formula bottles and diapers. She should be writing this down.

"She'll probably sleep for another half hour or so," Lois said while gingerly helping Hank into his coat. The man was clearly in agony. "Samuel's on his way to Austin to pick up some fencing material, so he won't be back until early afternoon. I can't say for sure how long we'll be."

Joella fought to conceal her growing panic. Why had she agreed to do this? "Don't worry about a thing," she heard herself saying. "We'll get along fine."

Lois slid her purse strap onto her shoulder. "Arturo's in his study," she said, lowering her voice. "We told him you were coming over to help *him* take care of Sophie, so, um, maybe just play along?"

"Of course. Whatever you say."

"And don't mention the party," Lois added in a stage whisper.

Joella helped Lois guide Hank's wheelchair out the door, then ease him into the back seat of her sedan. A few minutes later, alone in the quiet house, she wandered to the living room, where Sophie slept in an old-style bassinet trimmed with a blue gingham skirt. One end of the skirt bore the name *Samuel* embroidered in large, navy-blue block letters. There must be a similar bassinet stored somewhere with Spencer's name, and Lois probably couldn't wait for the opportunity to bring it out for her other son's firstborn.

Did Lindsey know about the bassinets? After her parents divorced, Lindsey had always insisted she'd never have kids and risk putting them through the heartache she'd suffered. Had she changed her mind now that she'd found true love with Spencer?

Would true love ever be enough to change Joella's mind about the risks of developing Alzheimer's—even worse, passing along the gene to children of her own?

The creak of a floorboard drew her attention. Arturo stood at the living room door, a scowl on his face. "What are you doing here?"

He might be small of stature, but the menacing tone of his voice left no room for doubting his authority. Joella pasted on a nervous smile. "Hi, Mr. Navarro. I'm Joella James. Lois asked me to come over and..." How to say this tactfully? "And see if you needed a hand watching Sophie while they're gone."

At the mention of Sophie, Arturo's expression gentled. He strode over to the bassinet and peered lovingly at the sleeping baby. "Ah, *mi* Sarita. She rests so peacefully." Sighing, he turned toward Joella, and his forehead wrinkled with confusion. "Who did you say you are?"

She told him again, and he nodded as if trying to understand, but he still looked bewildered. No wonder Lois had concerns about leaving the baby in his care.

Just then, Sophie began to squirm and whimper. Before Joella could intervene, Arturo scooped up the baby and snuggled her against his chest. "There, there, little one. Papi's got you."

Worried he'd lose his balance and drop the baby, Joella hovered close. She motioned toward the glider. "Why don't you sit and rock her?"

Arturo made his way to the chair, and Joella kept one hand on his elbow as he lowered himself into the seat. “You aren’t being paid to fuss over me,” he snapped. “Make yourself useful and warm Sarita’s bottle.”

So he thought she was hired help? Probably safer than knowing she lived and worked next door at the McClement ranch.

And *Sarita*? Was that his pet name for Sophie? It must mean something special in Spanish. Joella would have to ask Lois about it later.

In the kitchen, she found Sophie’s formula bottles in the fridge and set one in the warmer according to Lois’s instructions. So far, so good. Now, had Lois said to change the baby’s diaper before or after feeding her? *If only you’d done more babysitting as a teenager, you might know some of this stuff.*

Instead, she was learning on the fly. And dare she admit she was a teensy bit excited about it? Try as she might to resist falling in love with the baby girl in the next room, Sophie was already working her charms.

Oh, dear, she *would* take after her handsomely charming daddy!

Samuel came away from his chat with the Rolling Hills Quarter Horses ranch manager with a headful of information and the certainty that, technologically speaking, Navarro Quarter Horses had fallen far behind the times. But would his father trust him to bring the ranch up to date?

Or would both Dad and Tito continue to hold his previous lack of interest in the family business against him?

It was nearing three o'clock when he arrived home and parked beside the supply barn. A couple of ranch hands came over to start unloading the corral panels.

"Can you take it from here?" Samuel asked as he shoved the sliding barn door open. "I need to check on things at the house."

"Your parents aren't back yet," one of the men answered.

"Not back from where?"

"You haven't heard? Your dad took a turn for the worse. They've gone to see a doctor."

Samuel's stomach twisted. He tugged his phone from his pocket and dialed his mother's number. While the phone rang in his ear, Samuel jogged toward the house. He was worried about his dad, sure, but he also needed to know who'd been taking care of Sophie all this time.

Mom finally answered. "Sorry I didn't call, honey. I didn't realize how long we'd be here. They had to make sure your dad's broken rib hadn't caused more serious internal damage."

"Is he going to be okay?" He'd reached the back door and was breathing almost as hard as he had on his run with Joella that morning.

"He will be. The doctor gave him something stronger for the pain, along with a stern lecture about resting as much as possible. We should be on our way home soon."

"That's great, but…where's Sophie?"

His mother chuckled softly. "In good hands, I promise. She's at the house with Joella and your grandfather."

With Joella? Samuel paused inside the screen porch. "Okay, well…tell Dad everything went fine in Austin. See you soon." With a quick goodbye, he hurried inside.

From the living room came Tito's raspy voice rising and falling in a lilting melody. The words were in Spanish, and it sounded like a lullaby. *"Duerme pequeña, no tengas temor. Descansa a salvo en los brazos de tu papi."—Sleep, little one, don't be afraid. Rest safely in your daddy's arms.*

Warmth spread through Samuel's chest as he noticed yet again how different Tito seemed around Sophie. When the old man held her, his gruffness vanished, revealing an unexpectedly tender side of his nature. Samuel hung his jacket and baseball cap on the hook beside the back door, then quietly made his way to the living room.

Joella sat on the sofa with a small pile of baby clothes in her lap and a neatly folded stack beside her. She looked up with surprise. "Oh, hi." She lowered her voice. "Did you get the word about your dad?"

"Just spoke with Mom. They should be on their way soon." Samuel's gaze was riveted on Tito as he cradled and rocked Sophie. The old man barely acknowledged Samuel and continued his gentle singing.

"Kind of amazing, isn't it?" Joella murmured. "He's hardly let her out of his sight all day."

Samuel eased around the coffee table and took a seat at the other end of the sofa. "Have you been here the whole time?"

Heaving a tired sigh, she nodded. "He thinks I'm a paid sitter. I've been relegated to bottle warming and diaper changes." She finished folding a pink bunny-print sleeper and laid it on the stack. "Oh, and laundering baby clothes."

Tito's lullaby segued into a low, rumbling snore, and now both he and the baby were snoozing in the glider. Samuel couldn't help grinning at the endearing picture they made. Then, realizing Joella had been kept from her work all day, he stood. "I'll take over now. You're probably ready to get out of here."

Laying the last of the baby clothes beside her, she pushed up from the sofa and stretched. "It's been a pleasant day, actually. Your grandfather's a pretty nice guy when he wants to be."

"Sophie has brought out the best in him." And in Joella, too, by the looks of things. Samuel could hardly believe this was the same woman who'd rushed out the other day as if she couldn't escape the baby fast enough.

In the kitchen, she took her sweater and shoulder bag from the coatrack, then turned with a thoughtful smile. "The nickname he calls her—Sarita—does it mean something special?"

"Yeah, I've heard him use it lately, too. It's a Spanish form of *Sarah*, which means *princess*. So he's calling her his 'little princess.'"

"That's sweet. He sure treats her like one." She smiled her thanks as Samuel helped her get her sweater on. "I'm a little concerned about your mother, though. She seemed pretty stressed when she called me this morning."

"The last couple of weeks have taken a toll." He winced. "And I only added to the stress by showing up with a baby no one expected."

Her expression tensed slightly, but she offered an understanding nod. "If I can help like this again, please ask."

Samuel's brows shot up. "After the other day, I had the feeling you weren't—I mean—"

"Right, another embarrassing moment I'd rather forget." She glanced away, looking anywhere but at him. "When I held Sophie that first time, so many confusing emotions welled up inside, and I didn't know how to deal with them."

The sudden and surprising urge to comfort her was irresistible. He lightly touched her arm. "If you ever need to talk about anything…"

A tentative smile returning, she met his gaze. "I'm working on some personal matters, but getting away from the city and coming here to Gabriel Bend is…well, I know it's going to help me come to terms with everything."

Those were feelings Samuel could relate to. "There's definitely something about small-town country living. Never thought I'd find myself back on the ranch, but you can't predict where the Lord's going to lead you."

Joella's eyes narrowed in a curious look, as if his reference to God had caught her off guard. "Like they say, the Lord works in mysterious ways."

Mysterious indeed. Spencer had suggested he talk to Joella about baby care, but could her actually making the offer be the solution he'd been praying for? He scraped a hand across the back of his neck. "Did you mean it about helping with Sophie if I needed someone?"

"Yes." She drew the word out as her brows slanted upward.

"The thing is, my mother needs a break. She's been watching Sophie in the mornings, and I'm taking her to the office with me after lunch. But getting a handle on ranch management is taking all my concentration, and when Sophie needs attention, everything comes to a screeching halt and I—" He realized his voice was rising as he spoke faster and faster. Stopping himself, he shrugged. "Sorry, I've been a little overwhelmed."

"It's okay. I get it." Watching him, Joella gnawed her lower lip. "Most of my event planning can be attended to in the mornings. Would it help if I came over for a couple of hours in the afternoons?"

He nearly collapsed with gratitude and relief. "You'd be saving my life—and my mom's."

"I could start tomorrow, say around two o'clock?"

He jumped on her offer before she could back out, and they made plans for her to meet him and Sophie at the apartment. Once he showed her where everything was and got them settled, he'd head down to the office. And if Joella ran into any problems or questions, he'd be close enough to run up and help.

An agreement reached, Joella said her goodbyes. As Samuel watched her from the window, tingles shot through his chest, the sensation so strong that his breath caught. They still weren't exactly *friends*—this was more of a neighbor-helping-neighbor situation—but something about Joella drew him in a way he'd never experienced with Chelsea, and they'd made a baby together. Of course, he'd never once imagined himself in love with Chelsea. The person he'd been then was only out for a good time, with no thought for the future, much less for who might get hurt.

Could Joella really believe he was still *that guy*? After their time together in the hayloft, when he'd never so much as written or called after she'd returned home at the end of summer vacation, she must have been both confused and hurt. Now he was a single father with a sordid past.

Would anything convince her he'd changed?

Pausing on the driveway, Joella looked toward the road, then decided to take the shorter route and headed toward the old gap in the barbed-wire fence. She ducked through the opening and started across the field, her strides purposeful despite the fatigue creeping into her bones. When Lois had pleaded for her help, she hadn't expected to be left alone with Arturo and the baby most of the day.

On the other hand, she hadn't lied when she'd told Samuel it had been a pleasant experience. True, the first hour or so had been awkward, in no small part because of Arturo's bossiness but also because even to look at Sophie evoked a yearning so strong that her chest ached.

They'd soon settled into a Sophie-dictated routine, though. The sweet little thing couldn't care less about Joella's futile longings, and Arturo was oblivious.

But volunteering to watch Sophie on a regular basis? That had certainly come out of nowhere. Yet she wasn't sorry. Things had gone amazingly well today, well enough that she'd been able to stuff away her guilt over the near-tragedy in Dallas. Besides, if any problems arose, Samuel would be right downstairs.

She could do this. She really could.

Reaching the back porch, she sank onto the top step. Though she'd enjoyed her time with Sophie, something about Arturo had been nagging at her all day. One thing she'd noticed—Samuel and Spencer always called him Tito, short for *abuelito, grandfather*. But when he was singing or whispering to the baby, he referred to himself as *Papi*, Spanish for *Daddy*.

It must be his great-grandfather pet name, that was all, unless…

She massaged her forehead. Could Arturo be showing signs of senility? At almost ninety years old, it wouldn't be unusual, but if so, how much had the family noticed?

The kitchen door opened. Looking concerned, Lindsey came out and plopped down next to Joella. "You look exhausted."

"It's more mental than physical. I'm not used to babysitting octogenarians and newborns, and definitely not at the same time."

Lindsey scoffed. "I can't even imagine spending hours on end with Arturo. Sophie, on the other hand…" Her gaze turned dreamy. "I'm still not sure if or when I'll be ready to be a mom, but being around Sophie definitely has me thinking about it. In the meantime, I'll soon have my hands full babysitting our spring calves."

"Any births yet?"

"Not so far, but one of the heifers has been acting restless. Audra's keeping a close eye on her. First-time moms are the most concerning, because they have no idea what's happening."

Joella's thoughts flew to Samuel and how unprepared he must have felt at suddenly finding himself a first-time dad. True, it was his own fault, but perhaps fatherhood might be what it took to tame the once wild Samuel Navarro. She'd like to believe he'd changed, and the way he'd spoken about God's leading certainly made her wonder.

Lindsey narrowed her eyes at Joella. "Hmm, I've only ever seen that look on your face when you were thinking about a boy."

Embarrassed, she sat straighter. "I—I was just thinking how cute Sophie is."

"Sophie…or her handsome daddy?"

"Don't even go there." Joella shoved up from the step. "I am so behind on my work today. I'd better go make some calls."

Keeping busy was the only real antidote for wandering thoughts, especially when Lindsey's not-so-subtle reference to Samuel hit pretty much on target. *What's going on, God? Both Samuel* and *his precious baby? Why would You purposefully place temptation right in front of me when You know what I've been through… what I'd risk by giving in?*

She spent the remainder of the afternoon working on the arrangements for Nora Nicolson's sixteenth birthday party, coming up in less than a month. If there was anyone in the Gabriel Bend area she needed to impress with her event planning skills, certainly the mayor and her family qualified.

The next morning was more of the same, including going over Mrs. Nicolson's menu choices with Holly and cornering Lindsey between ranch chores to brainstorm decorations and party favors.

Then around noon, Lois called to say she'd been going over the guest list for Arturo's party, and the number kept growing. "He's acquainted with just about everybody in the county, it seems—plus all his *charro* buddies from the old days. I'm getting worried the old barn won't have room enough to handle everyone. Think you and Samuel could figure something out in case we need extra space?"

"Creating extra space out of thin air is part of my job." Joella blew a strand of hair out of her eyes, then checked the time. "I'll be coming over soon to watch Sophie. While I'm there, maybe I can take another look at the barn and surrounding area."

"Samuel told me you'd offered to babysit in the afternoons. That'll be such a huge help, for all of us."

"My pleasure."

Joella crossed off a few more items from her to-do list, then took a lunch break. Afterward, she scurried upstairs to tug on socks and lace up her sneakers. Except for appointments with clients, jeans and fuzzy slippers had become her go-to office attire since she'd moved to the ranch. She tucked her planner, cell phone and fifty-foot measuring tape into her tote and headed across the field to the Navarros'.

As she crossed the driveway, Samuel emerged from the main barn, Sophie snuggled in his arms. "Well, Tito's party is no longer a surprise. He overheard Mom on the phone with you and started asking a bunch of questions."

"Uh-oh. I hope he's excited about it."

"That's a major understatement. He immediately took over the invitation list, so I have a feeling the head count's about to grow exponentially. Mom said you wanted another look at the barn. Is now okay?"

"Let's go. I'm thinking if there's room, we could erect a party tent either in front of or beside the barn." Her elbow accidentally brushed his, sending a shiver up her arm. She subtly increased the distance between them. "By the way, how's your dad doing?"

"He's feeling a lot better since the new pain meds kicked in. He's supposed to take it easy, but keeping him on bed rest is proving a challenge. In our family, obstinacy is definitely an inherited trait."

She'd leave that remark alone. "It's good he has you and Spencer to depend on."

Samuel scoffed. "Not sure he feels the same way, at least where I'm concerned."

The discouragement in his tone evoked a wave of compassion. "But you're here. Surely your father appreciates what you gave up to come home to the ranch."

"Maybe." He kissed his baby's head as she dozed on his shoulder. "But I also had selfish reasons."

"I don't think it's selfish to lean on your family when you need them." If only her parents had relied more on her as they struggled with Mom's illness.

They'd reached the barn. A perfect time to change the subject. "There should be plenty of room here in front for a party tent." She pulled the measuring tape from her tote and handed the end to Samuel. "Let's see exactly what we have to work with."

After jotting some dimensions in her notebook, she nodded. "I'm thinking we can seat at least eighty inside the barn, and another sixty or eighty out here under a tent. It'll work out fine, unless your grandfather really does plan on inviting the whole county."

Samuel laughed. "Wouldn't put it past him. But we'll try to keep it under control."

"Good, because we'll also need to plan for parking."

"We could create access to one of the nearby pastures."

"That would work." Turning to a new page in her planner, Joella made a rough sketch of the barn and surrounding areas. "Okay, that's all I need for now. Ready to get me settled in with Sophie for the afternoon?"

Chapter Five

As Samuel led the way up to the apartment, Sophie began whimpering for her next bottle. “Talk about good timing.”

Joella followed him to the kitchenette. “Just show me where everything is, and I’ll take over so you can get to work.”

Yesterday this had seemed like a practical solution. Now Samuel was having second thoughts. Not that he didn’t trust his baby with Joella, but the arrangement felt extremely lopsided. She had her own business to run. How could he justify accepting free babysitting from her?

“I really appreciate this.” He took a formula bottle from the fridge. “The temporary nanny I’d hired in Houston charged fifteen dollars an hour. Does that sound fair for you?”

She speared him with an icy glare. “Being

paid never so much as occurred to me, and I'm insulted you would even suggest it."

Sophie's cries were becoming more insistent. Bouncing her gently, Samuel set the bottle in the warmer. "You said you wanted to keep things professional between us. I didn't want to take advantage, that's all."

"If I thought you were, I'd say so." She held out her arms. "Here, let me take her before you give her whiplash."

He didn't think he'd been jostling Sophie that hard, but in his distracted state, he may have overdone it a bit. Frowning, he handed the baby to Joella, then uncapped the bottle and passed it to her. "If I offended you, I apologize."

"Apology accepted." With the baby cradled in her arms, Joella offered the bottle. "Now, where can I find Sophie's things?"

Samuel gave a curt nod before leading her to the storage-closet-turned-nursery. "Diapers and wipes are in the top drawer, clothes and clean blankets below. She's supposed to sleep on her back, not her stomach—"

"That much I know."

Jaw clenched, he took a couple of calming breaths before turning to face her. "I still have a lot to learn, but I'm sure it can't be good for a baby's well-being if her father and her caregiver are at odds."

"You're right," she said softly, her gaze fixed on Sophie. "It's my turn to apologize. I shouldn't take my personal issues out on you."

"Which begs the question, do those *personal issues* have anything to do with me?"

Joella glanced up, then away, her silence speaking volumes. Oblivious, Sophie continued nursing.

With whatever this was hanging between them, Samuel couldn't possibly go down to the office and hope to concentrate on work. He took a clean burp cloth from one of the drawers and motioned toward the living room. "I think we'd better sit down and clear the air."

Still holding Sophie, Joella eased into the rocking chair. Tension in every limb, Samuel opted to remain standing. He paced to the front windows and back while searching for the best way to begin.

Except...she looked so *right* sitting there in his living room with his baby in her arms.

Shake it off, Navarro. Keep your head on straight.

He halted a few feet away and cleared his throat. "I spent a lot of years rebelling against what others expected of me—everything from joining the family business to embracing the biblical values my parents worked so hard to instill. So I get that I have a lot to make up for. All I ask is that you judge me on who I am today, not the man—or the impetuous kid—I used to be."

The sudden clenching of her jaw said his last remark had hit a nerve. "I'm trying, Samuel. But I can't forget—" Eyes filling, she clamped down on her lower lip. "After…after we were together in the hayloft that night, I spent the next two months worried I might be pregnant." Inhaling deeply, she whispered, "Thank God I wasn't."

Renewed shame squeezed his gut. He pulled his hand down his face and sank onto the sofa. "I'm so sorry, Joella. I never thought—"

"Exactly. You *never thought*." The disappointment in her eyes pierced his heart. "You made me believe you cared. Then after I went home, you never even called or wrote."

"I *did* care, and I thought you did, too." He glanced away. "I know it was wrong the way I let things drop. But summer was ending and I… I guess I figured a clean break would be easier."

Sophie had finished her bottle. Joella set it on the end table, then lifted thc baby to her shoulder and patted her back. "I get it," she said through tight lips. "A teenage summer fling. What should I have expected?"

"I have no excuse for that night, and I'll forever regret hurting you. I mean it, Joella. I'm sorry."

She remained silent for so long that Samuel began to wonder if she'd ever speak to him again, much less forgive him. Using the back of her hand, she brushed the dampness from her cheeks. When she pressed a gentle kiss to Sophie's head, his heart twisted. What if she had had his baby? Would he have seen the light and turned his life around any sooner? Would he have been man enough to do the right thing?

"I accept your apology," she said at last. "Let's admit we were both at fault and leave it in the past."

He studied her. "Can you? I mean, it's felt like you've been judging me ever since I showed up with Sophie."

Again, she grew quiet, as if framing her next words carefully. "I just don't understand how you can carry on as if Sophie's mother doesn't exist. You made a baby together. You must have had feelings for her."

"I suppose I did, in a way. But neither of us would have called it love." How could he explain that part of his life when he didn't fully understand it himself? Dragging his fingers through his hair, he rose and strode to the window. "Competition in my office could get pretty cutthroat, so to relieve the stress, the colleagues I hung out with, including Chelsea, got heavy into drinking and partying. When Chelsea and I started dating, she was on the rebound after breaking up with a real jerk, and our relationship heated up fast. But as messed up as we both were, it wasn't long before things started getting ugly. We argued over little things, and then bigger things, and then she accused me of sabotaging a deal she'd been negotiating."

"Did you do it?"

"No, but the repercussions nearly got me kicked out of the firm. That, followed by our volatile breakup, scared me enough that I knew I had to get myself straightened out—on every level. A week later, Chelsea left the company. I never knew about the pregnancy until her attorney contacted me barely over two weeks ago to tell me about Sophie." He blew out a lengthy sigh. "Even after all we'd been through, all the hurt we caused each other, she decided I'd be the best one to raise our daughter."

He turned to find Joella wearing a thoughtful frown as she gently rocked Sophie. "Lindsey told me about the letter Chelsea left you, but I didn't know the whole story. Obviously, I made assumptions."

Head tilted, he gave a weak shrug. "Considering my history—*our* history—how can I blame you?"

"Well, I'm sorry. If I'd been paying attention instead of letting old hurts get in the way, I'd have realized how much you've changed."

"Thank you," he murmured, his chest warming. "Hearing you say that means a lot."

"So. Shouldn't you be getting back to work?" Her tone was all business again, but the essence of a smile lurked behind the words. "Go on. We'll be fine."

Grateful relief flooded him. When he bent to drop a kiss on his baby's head, his temple brushed against Joella's hair. His senses filled with a pleasant mix of Sophie's lavender baby lotion and Joella's honeysuckle-scented shampoo.

"Okay, then." Clearing his throat, he straightened abruptly. "I'm right downstairs if you need anything."

It felt good to finally have things out in the open, at least where Samuel was concerned. As for other parts of her life, Joella intended to keep those private. For as long as she could do her job and do it well, she refused to place herself under constant scrutiny, much less be pitied by her closest friends.

The incident with the toddler *had* to be a freak accident, didn't it? Nothing either before or since had come close to matching the gravity of that error. Besides, the symptoms of early-onset Alzheimer's didn't typically appear until age forty or fifty. She had a good ten years yet—longer, God willing. In the meantime, she intended to do everything possible to keep her brain sharp.

There was always the option of getting a genetic test, but even though a negative result might bring a measure of reassurance, it couldn't guarantee she'd *never* develop dementia. Nor would a positive result mean she absolutely would be stricken with the disease. Ultimately, she'd come to prefer *not* knowing the percentages.

Slamming the door on such futile thinking, she focused on the precious pink bundle in her arms. "Let's get your diaper changed, sweet thing."

With Sophie tucked into her crib for a nap, Joella retrieved her notebook and reviewed the plans for Arturo's party. She made a couple of calls she hadn't gotten to that morning and checked more items off her to-do list. Sophie was still sleeping when Samuel returned around four forty-five.

"How'd it go?" he asked, glancing around.

"Not a peep since I laid her down right after you left." She wouldn't admit she'd looked in on the sleeping baby every fifteen minutes to verify she was still breathing.

Samuel peeked into the nursery, then turned to Joella with a sheepish smile. "Several times a night I wake up anxious and check to make sure she's okay."

Joella nodded and smiled. Nice to know she wasn't alone. "I'll be going, then." She gathered up her things. "Same time tomorrow?"

"If that works for you. And, ah..." He tweaked his beard. "I'm hoping to get in another run in the morning, if you're interested."

She shrugged. "Running with a friend would definitely make it easier to drag myself out of bed at six a.m."

Samuel's boyish grin pulled her back to the summer she was sixteen all over again. "I'll be waiting for you, *friend*."

Great. Her fault for letting the word slip out. But *friendship*? With *Samuel*? Who was she kidding, when his mere glance could make her heart race like this?

She'd better get these feelings under control, and quickly, because being his friend and spending time with his baby had to be enough.

The next morning, she met him as he jogged in place at the end of the McClement driveway. They made it a little farther this time before easing to a walk. Joella surmised Samuel could have maintained his faster pace much longer but purposely slowed to accommodate her. Her traitorous heart didn't seem to mind one bit.

By the time she walked next door to watch Sophie for the afternoon, she'd corralled her wayward emotions. Samuel seemed much more relaxed as he left the baby in her care, and after yesterday's success, both at clearing the air and getting familiar with Sophie's routine, Joella felt much more comfortable, too. The newborn's needs were simple—feeding, changing, snuggling, napping. The most important thing was being on hand when she needed attention, which Joella was happy to give. In only a few short days, she'd fallen head over heels in love with this sweet baby girl.

Everything went smoothly on Thursday afternoon as well. When Samuel came upstairs, Joella had just given Sophie a bottle and was pacing the sitting area with her while waiting for a burp. She released a loud one as Samuel walked in, and he and Joella both gave a surprised laugh.

"Wow," he said, crossing the room, "I never knew such a big noise could come out of such a tiny body."

The closer he came, the faster Joella's pulse throbbed. So much for keeping her feelings in check. "I was about to change her diaper and rock her for a few minutes. Would you rather—" Her cell phone chimed from inside her tote, where she'd left it on the sofa. She cast Samuel a look of apology. "I should probably answer. I've been waiting for a callback from a vendor."

He held out his arms for Sophie. "Go ahead. I'll take over."

Joella retrieved her phone and checked the display. "Oh, it's the mayor. Her daughter's party is coming up soon." She scooped up her tote and moved toward the door as she answered. "Hello, Mayor Nicolson. What can I do—"

"You can return my deposit, that's what." The woman sounded incensed.

Joella's stomach twisted. "I—I don't understand."

"I just got off the phone with a very good friend of mine in Dallas. She was at the party where you almost let a toddler die."

It took an act of will to keep from doubling over. Bile crept up her throat, and she struggled to swallow. "It was an honest oversight. I didn't know—"

"And that's the problem. It was your job to know your client's child had a life-threatening peanut allergy." The mayor released an angry huff. "Under the circumstances, I cannot possibly put my daughter and her friends at risk. I'm firing you, Ms. James, and I'll expect a full refund of all monies paid to you thus far."

The line went dead.

With Sophie cradled in one arm, Samuel rushed to Joella's side. He caught her phone an instant before it would have hit the floor. "Hey, take a breath. What happened?"

"How could I be so stupid?" she muttered. "Why did I ever think it would all just go away?"

He guided her back to the sofa. "Wait here while I lay Sophie down. I'll be right back."

The baby was already drifting off as he placed her in the crib. He pulled the door partway closed, then returned to the living room, where Joella sat trembling on the edge of the sofa. He eased down next to her and drew her beneath the shelter of his embracc. She collapsed against him, and as he murmured soothing words to her, he couldn't resist bestowing a kiss to her temple. "It's okay, it's okay."

After a moment, she shuddered and straightened, hands covering her eyes. "How many times now have I fallen apart in front of you? You must really think I'm losing it."

"I think there's more you're holding in that you need to open up about." His arm hadn't left her shoulder, but he already missed the warmth of her side against his. "Talk to me, Joella. What happened with Mayor Nicolson?"

She released a long, pained sigh. "She's canceling her daughter's birthday party and wants all her money back."

Samuel took a few seconds to process the news. "We know the Nicolsons. Our families have been attending the same church for years. It's not like them to pull out of a commitment without good reason."

"Oh, she had a good reason, all right." Bitterness laced Joella's tone. "She found out why I left my corporate event planning job in Dallas and doesn't want me anywhere near her daughter."

"What are you talking about?" He gently shifted her around to face him. "Joella, tell me. It can't be that bad."

"Not that bad?" Face contorted, she met his gaze. "Because of my mistake, my client's two-year-old daughter came close to dying from anaphylactic shock. I somehow missed that she had a peanut allergy, and one of the desserts the caterer served contained peanut butter."

Samuel's stomach knotted as he imagined the parent's terror. If something like that ever happened to Sophie... "But it was an accident, right? How was it your fault?"

"Because it should have been in the file. With every client, I routinely make a note of any concerning health or safety issues, including—and especially—food allergies. Only this one time..." Her voice broke, and she looked away. "I failed."

He wasn't sure what to say, how to help. And who was he to offer reassurance anyway after the mistakes he'd made?

Joella rose and took a few halting steps away before turning. "You should certainly tell your family about this, and if they want to fire me from your grandfather's party, I will completely understand. In the meantime, I have some explaining to do with Holly and Lindsey...and possibly some suitcases to pack."

"Don't jump to conclusions—about my parents or about your best friends." He stood and gripped her arms. "People can be more forgiving than you give them credit for. Believe me, I speak from personal experience."

"Sophie." Her eyes flew open. She shook her head vehemently. "You should never have entrusted me with her care. I'd simply die if anything happened to her because of something I did...or failed to do."

"Enough of that kind of talk." He tried not to visibly react, but he couldn't deny the misgivings already tunneling through his thoughts. "I know you'd never hurt my daughter."

"Not intentionally, no. But if—if—" She pressed a fist to her mouth to stifle a sob.

He hated seeing her in such distress, and the urge to hold and comfort her became irresistible. Gently, he enfolded her in his arms and tucked her head against his chest. When she hiccuped softly and snuggled deeper, a surge of long-stifled emotions rushed through him.

As if sensing his feelings, she heaved a shaky sigh and pulled away. "Thank you for the reassurance, but this is my mess, and I'll deal with it."

"Joella..."

With a dismissive wave, she grabbed her things and darted out the door.

He stood frozen as he waited for his pounding pulse to slow. The feelings he'd experienced holding Joella had staggered him with their intensity. He was still attracted to her, no doubt about it, but this was *not* the right time, for either of them. Joella had some serious difficulties to unravel, and he was still figuring out what his future held as a single dad.

On top of it all, he found himself questioning whether he could safely allow Joella to continue caring for Sophie. He'd witnessed firsthand the growing attachment between the two of them, and he could never in a million years bring himself to sever that bond. For his own peace of mind and out of respect and concern for Joella, he had to find a way to fix this.

Back in the office the next morning, he turned his attention to his other pressing goal—showing his father that he could pull his weight as the ranch's office manager. He'd been reading up on the software AJ Bell had told him about, but since their outdated computer wouldn't be compatible, investing in a new system couldn't be put off. Convincing Dad would be a challenge, though, so earlier that week, deciding he'd fare better if he asked forgiveness rather than permission, he'd placed the order. If necessary, he'd forgo his own salary for a month or two.

While he waited for the sluggish computer to wake up, his thoughts shifted once more to Joella and what she'd told him about the incident with the toddler. If he could unearth more details, perhaps even prove Joella hadn't been fully at fault, maybe he could put both her mind and his own to rest.

Once he got online, he looked up the number of city hall. Word spread fast around Gabriel Bend, and it wouldn't take much for Mayor Nicolson to derail any chance of success for River Bend Events. He dialed the number and got transferred a couple of times before the mayor finally came on the line.

"Well, hello, Samuel. It was good to see you with your family in church last Sunday. How's your father doing after his horrible accident?"

"Improving every day, thanks." He combed his fingers through his hair and strove for a casual tone. "I just called to let you know you should be getting an invitation soon for my grandfather's ninetieth birthday."

"Wonderful! That should be quite the celebration."

"Yes, our event planner is already hard at work on it. Say, I heard Nora's got a birthday coming up, too."

"She'll be sixteen the end of the month. We were planning a big party, but all that's fallen through. I sincerely hope—" The mayor's voice hardened. "But of course you must be using River Bend Events, since your new sister-in-law is one of the owners. I'd seriously advise you to rethink that choice."

Samuel paused for effect. "If this is about Joella James, I'm aware there was an issue with a previous client."

"Whose child almost died! The woman should be banned from the business entirely."

"Mrs. Nicolson, Joella is a family friend. I can't believe she'd ever intentionally risk the safety of a client or anyone else."

"Intentional or not, she was careless, and I refuse to have her anywhere near my daughter or her friends."

This was getting nowhere. Samuel stifled his frustration and calmly asked, "Are you sure you have all the facts?"

"My friend in Dallas who attended the event seemed quite certain about what transpired."

"Do you think your friend would mind a call from me to ask a few questions?" Careful with his choice of words, he continued, "Since Joella is arranging my grandfather's party, you're right—it pays to be cautious."

"Wise choice. Do give Sharon a call." She gave him her friend's name and number. "I'll text her right now to let her know she'll be hearing from you."

As he thanked the mayor and said goodbye, his father limped in on his crutches. "You need to get busy inventorying supplies for the foaling barn. We're running out of time."

"I know, Dad. I've been working on it and should finish today. And since you're here… I really need us to talk more about those computer upgrades I've been pushing for."

Chapter Six

Much as she'd like to, Joella couldn't put off telling Holly and Lindsey about the mayor's cancellation. If only she could have awakened the next morning to discover it was all a bad dream.

She stalled until nearly lunchtime while they worked through other business. Then Holly brought up Nora Nicolson's party. "It's three weeks away, and I need some clarification about the menu. Joella, have you heard any more from the mayor this week?"

She hauled in a breath and released it slowly. "There's no easy way to say this. The party's off."

"What?" Holly's mouth fell open.

Lindsey's expression mirrored Holly's. "They *canceled*? Why?"

Joella buried her face in her hands. "I'm

sorry. It's entirely my fault. I'll cover the losses."

Her friends rounded the table, one on either side of her. "Honey, it's okay," Lindsey soothed. "We're in this together."

"Absolutely. Just tell us what happened." Holly patted Joella's back.

With a pained sigh, she straightened. "It all goes back to why I left my Dallas job. I never told you the whole story, so…maybe you'd better sit down."

Concern etched in every line of their faces, Holly and Lindsey retreated to chairs on the opposite side of the table. They sat with stunned expressions as Joella told them how the toddler's peanut allergy had been missed during menu planning, and only the quick use of an EpiPen had averted tragedy.

"So Mayor Nicolson is right," she finished, rubbing her eyes. "She shouldn't trust me, and neither should you or Samuel or anyone else."

"That is *so* not true," Lindsey blurted. "It could have happened anywhere."

"It doesn't excuse the fact that I should have made sure the caterer and her crew were informed. It was my error."

"No," came a masculine voice from the hall. It sounded like Spencer, but when he burst into the room, the citified pullover and jeans confirmed it was Samuel. "No, Joella," he repeated, "it wasn't."

She could only stare at him and shake her head. All the reassurance in the world couldn't change what she'd let happen. Why had she ever thought things would be better here? It was bad enough she'd jeopardized Holly's and Lindsey's futures by partnering with them. She'd already made up her mind to tell Samuel today that she would no longer babysit for him.

Oh, Sophie, how I'm going to miss you!

But Samuel just kept standing there, a crooked grin lighting his face. "I came straight over because I wanted to tell you in person." He glanced at Holly and Lindsey. "It's something you'll all want to hear. Joella, I contacted your former boss this morning."

"You...you what? Why?"

"Because my gut told me there had to be more to the story, and I was right. I convinced her to dig a little deeper, and she found the proof right there in the files."

Joella's head was spinning. "I don't understand. Found what?"

"A memo to the caterer signed by you that clearly stated *no peanut products* because the client's child was severely allergic." He thrust a sheet of paper toward her. "See for yourself. Your ex-boss emailed me a copy."

Scanning the page, she nodded, now recalling vividly the day she'd prepared the memo. In situations like this, she always flagged such notices with a big neon sticky note and placed them at the front of the client's file. But she'd been juggling a heavy schedule that week and had leaned heavily on Macy, her assistant, to make sure nothing fell through the cracks. She couldn't recall for the life of her if the memo had been there when she'd passed the folder to Macy to complete the digital file updates before forwarding to the caterer.

Brow furrowed, she looked up at Samuel. "Where did this turn up?"

"In a jumble of papers on your former assistant's desk. By the way, she just got fired."

Joella groaned. She felt awful that now Macy, too, had lost her job over this. The girl was smart and capable, but how many times had Joella chided her about needing to be more organized? Even so, she couldn't shift all the blame. "It was my client and my responsibility. I should have double-checked everything."

"Remember, I came from a corporate environment, too," Lindsey stated, "and if you can't delegate, what's the point of having a staff? So I won't let you keep beating yourself up over this when you should have been able to trust your assistant to do her job."

A part of her knew Lindsey was right, and an even bigger part relished the relief of knowing that, at least until she'd passed the file to Macy, everything had been in order. She cast Samuel a sheepish smile. "I can't believe you went to so much trouble to clear this up for me. Thank you."

Holding her gaze, he smiled back. "I also took the liberty of explaining the situation to Mayor Nicolson. She should be calling you shortly."

Joella brushed at the tear escaping down her cheek. "I—I don't know what to say. Or how to thank you."

"I have a few ideas," Holly said with a wink. "None of which have anything to do with talking. Lindsey, don't you have some cows to tend to?"

"Oh, right." Lindsey popped up from her chair. "And wasn't there a new recipe you were going to try out on us for lunch?"

Could her friends be any more obvious? Joella waited until they'd left the room, then came around the table to stand in front of Samuel. "Really, thank you. You have no idea what this means to me."

"I hated seeing you so upset yesterday, so I had to do something." He took her hand, turning it over in his own as if memorizing the shape of each finger. "You're a competent, confident woman. Don't ever doubt yourself."

"You're kind to say so, but you don't know…" Withdrawing her hand, she turned to retrieve her planning notebook. Better to hold on to something substantial than give over control to unspoken longings. "I'd already made up my mind to tell you. I don't think it's wise for me to continue watching Sophie."

"But why? I've just given you proof that what happened with the toddler wasn't your fault. Sophie needs you. We both—" his voice hitched "—need you."

Heart aching, she squeezed her eyes shut. It wouldn't be fair to bail on him on such short notice. "Okay, I'll come over this afternoon. But you should start looking into other arrangements."

Brow furrowed, he gave a weak shrug. "If that's what you want. But can we—"

Her phone, resting on the corner of the table, interrupted with a loud chime. Fumbling behind her, she snatched it up. "It's Mayor Nicolson. Excuse me. I should…"

"Right. I'll see you later." He backed toward the hallway, then turned and left.

Summoning a small measure of the confidence Samuel had praised her for only moments ago, she pressed the answer button. "Hello, Mayor Nicolson."

Hiking across the field, Samuel wondered what had just happened. Joella's spark of self-assurance, short-lived as it was, had been worth every minute he'd spent on the phone this morning convincing her former boss to dig deeper. After discovering the memo, the woman had expressed regret about demanding Joella's resignation, even suggesting she'd offer to rehire her.

Which was the absolute *last* thing Samuel wanted. His feelings for Joella were growing stronger than he dared admit, and he hated the possibility of her leaving Gabriel Bend. There'd been brief moments when he sensed she might still feel something for him as well.

Could that be part of the reason she'd concluded she couldn't continue watching Sophie? He'd thought after the other day that they'd put their teenage indiscretion behind them. Was she still hung up on the idea that he should have tried harder with Chelsea?

On his way to the barn office, he glimpsed Spencer leading a horse out of the training arena. Maybe his twin could offer a little perspective. Samuel waited for him at the barn door. "Good ride?"

"We have some work ahead of us, but she's showing a lot of promise." Spencer patted the mare's neck. "A delivery came while you were next door. It's obviously not feed or tack, so I had them put it in the office."

Had the new computer system Samuel had ordered—*without* telling his father—already arrived? Nervous perspiration popped out on his forehead. "Where's Dad now?"

Spencer nodded toward the office.

So much for that talk with his brother. Blowing sharply through the slit between his lips, Samuel steeled himself while mentally rehearsing the speech explaining his rationale he'd worked out in his head before placing the order.

Inside, his father balanced on his crutches as he stood over one of the open boxes. "I thought I made myself clear. A new computer isn't in the budget."

"I know, sir. But let me explain." Dad had shut him down pretty quickly every time he'd brought up the subject. Now, without getting too technical, he related his conversation with AJ Bell at Rolling Hills Quarter Horses. "Their management system impressed me, and I believe we could improve operations here considerably by implementing something similar—on a slightly smaller scale, of course."

Dad's expression hardened, as if he could look any more reproachful. "So the way we've been doing things isn't good enough for you?"

"It's not that. I just think a few key changes could make us more efficient." He peered into the larger box, his fingers itching to set up the new computer system and try it out. "Please, before you say no, give me a chance to show you what a newer method can do." *Give me a chance to prove myself!*

Dad didn't say anything for several interminable moments. Then, "I'm afraid to ask how much this cost."

"I put it on my own credit card for now, but give it time and it'll pay for itself. And until you're satisfied, don't pay me back."

"Don't tempt me." Giving his head a doubtful shake, Dad inched toward the door, then paused to say over his shoulder, "A shame you failed to put equal effort into how you conducted your personal affairs."

His dad's continual rejection of Sophie hurt deeply. Once the door clicked shut, he released a pent-up sigh. All he could do was continue praying Dad would forgive him and grow to love his granddaughter as much as Mom already did.

Returning his thoughts to thc task at hand, he began the process of backing up the old computer onto an external drive, then went to the house to see Sophie and have lunch with his parents. When Joella came over later, he could start setting up the new computer and copy over all the necessary programs and files. The barn management software AJ Bell had recommended had also come with the delivery. He was anxious to get it installed and begin importing the existing data from their antiquated spreadsheets.

He was on his way to the apartment with Sophie when Joella called his name. She strode across the driveway toward him, her golden hair tossed by the breeze and a red flannel overshirt flying out behind her like a superhero cape. Her expression was formidable… and she'd never looked more beautiful.

She halted in front of him, chin lifted. "Thank you again for what you did for me this morning. You saved River Bend Events from a quick and sure demise."

"I wouldn't go that far."

"No, I mean it." A strand of hair fluttered across her eyes. "If you hadn't gone to bat for us with the mayor, she could have done all kinds of damage to our credibility. I'd never have been able to forgive myself."

To keep from tucking the wayward strand behind her ear, he brushed his hand over Sophie's wispy curls instead, but his gaze kept straying to Joella's brow, her cheek, her lips.

Get a grip, he told himself, blinking rapidly. "I was just on my way up with Sophie. I was hoping we could talk more before I get back to work."

Her chin inched higher. "If you're hoping to change my mind about what I told you earlier, please don't try, because I—"

"Sam, Joella!" His mother's voice rang out from the back porch. "Glad I caught y'all before you go up. Can you come in and chat for a few minutes about the party?"

Joella couldn't help being grateful for the interruption. She didn't yet know how to explain to Samuel why she was backing out of their arrangement. Being vindicated in the toddler's near-tragedy had provided a brief glimmer of assurance. But, at least in her own mind, nothing Samuel had learned about the incident could fully absolve her.

If only she could live in the moment, trusting God day by day instead of constantly fearing what tomorrow would bring.

"Have a seat at the table," Lois said. "Care for some iced tea?"

"That would be great. Thanks."

Samuel pulled out a chair for her. "Mind holding Sophie while I help Mom?"

Her smile faltered, but she held out her arms. "Sure."

While Samuel and Lois filled glasses, Arturo ambled in. "There you are, my Sarita." He bent to stroke Sophie's wispy brown curls, then studied Joella. "Who are you?"

She reintroduced herself. "I was here a few days ago, remember? Helping you with the baby."

Nothing about his expression registered recognition. He thrust out his jaw. "I would remember such a thing. Now give her to me."

Samuel brought over a glass of tea and set it in front of Joella. "Tito, it's okay. I told her she could hold Sophie."

The man's eyes clouded. Mumbling something in Spanish, he wandered out of the kitchen.

"Sorry about that." Samuel gave a quick shake of his head. "When he's overtired, he sometimes gets confused."

It seemed more concerning than simple confusion, but glancing down at the warm little body snuggled in her arms, Joella found her gaze riveted once again by those precious plump cheeks and tiny rosebud lips.

Samuel pulled a chair closer, his smile widening as he glanced from the baby to Joella. "Look how she's looking at you."

The intensity in those round gray eyes made her shiver. "How can a newborn look so wise and all-knowing?"

"I know. It's like she can see all the way to your heart."

The funny catch in his voice drew Joella's attention, and now she was torn between soaking up Sophie's sweetness and succumbing to the charms of a man whose love for his daughter seeped from every pore.

"Ready to talk party business?" Lois's question ended Joella's reverie. "I think we've about firmed up the guest list, so I can give you some numbers."

"That's great." She turned her attention to Lois. "I understand Arturo found out about the party."

"Yes, and he's thrilled about it. Besides adding to the invitation list, he's also mentioned a few items he'd like on the menu."

Sophie began whimpering. "She's getting hungry," Samuel said. "I'll make a bottle and take her in the other room so you two can talk."

When Samuel hadn't returned by the time they'd wrapped up their discussion, Joella wondered if he'd forgotten she was there.

As she cast yet another glance toward the

doorway, Lois touched her arm. "He'll be back eventually. It just gets harder and harder to tear himself away from his baby girl."

Embarrassed that Lois had noticed her preoccupation, she faced forward and took a quick swallow of iced tea. "He's a good dad."

"I'm so proud of him. He's come a long way since..." Lois's words trailed off before she continued in a wistful tone, "Sometimes it takes losing our way before we can discover who we really are, and to learn that God is always waiting for us to come home."

Just then, Samuel strode in. Glancing at each of them in turn, he hiked a brow. "Why do I get the feeling y'all are talking about me behind my back?"

"Joella was just remarking what a good dad you are."

Cuddling the drowsing Sophie against his shoulder, he cast Joella a regretful smile. "Sorry, I'm supposed to be participating in the birthday plans, and I conveniently skipped out."

"It's okay. Your mom and I covered everything we needed to." She rose and carried her empty glass to the counter. "I'm sure you want to get back to work."

He grimaced. "Yeah, I need to get moving on my new project."

Lois narrowed her gaze at him. "A new computer system, huh? You're barely home two weeks and already upsetting your dad's apple cart." Her half grin and wink belied the accusation in her tone.

"About time somebody catapulted this ranch out of the dark ages."

"Just be careful you don't give your dad and grandfather whiplash."

Joella suffered a moment of envy at the friendly banter between Samuel and his mother. What she wouldn't give to have her parents back!

The thought brought an ache to her chest as the final months of her mother's life played across her mind. After the official Alzheimer's diagnosis, Mom had deteriorated rapidly. Protecting her dignity and her privacy, Dad had insisted on keeping her at home in familiar surroundings. The stress took an increasing toll on his health, and as the end neared, Joella had finally persuaded him to hire a private nurse. By then, Mom no longer recognized either her husband or her daughter.

Blinking away the memories, Joella realized both Samuel and Lois were staring at her with concern. She uttered a dismissive laugh. "Sorry, woolgathering again."

Samuel's skeptical frown said he guessed

there was more to it than wandering thoughts. Tucking Sophie's blanket around her, he opened the back door and waited for Joella to step out ahead of him.

As they crossed the back porch, she forestalled questions by asking one of her own. "What's this about a new computer system?"

Enthusiasm lighting his face, he told her about his meeting with another ranch manager. "Dad and Spencer may know horses, but computers and office management? Not so much. This is one area where I might actually be able to contribute."

Recalling his words to her earlier, she looked at him askance. "Maybe you should listen to your own advice about not doubting yourself."

"Thanks, but if I want the same level of respect my father and grandfather have for Spencer, I have to work ten times as hard to earn it."

"Why—because of your brother's horsemanship skills?" They'd paused on the driveway. "Your strengths may be different, but you're no less worthy of respect. You were successful in your real-estate career, weren't you? So I'm sure those business skills will serve you equally well in ranch management."

Head tilted, Samuel grinned. "You're pretty good at this pep-talk thing."

"For other people, yes." Joella sighed. "But like you, sometimes I need to take my own advice."

Upstairs in the apartment, Samuel placed Sophie in her crib while Joella arranged her planner, cell phone and laptop on the dining table. With the updates Lois had given her, she could make the necessary adjustments to Arturo's party arrangements and email the menu requests to Holly.

Samuel joined her at the table, his expression serious. "About babysitting…please tell me you'll reconsider. I'm not asking only because I'm desperate for the help. You're great with Sophie. I've seen how she responds to you, and it's obvious how much you care about her."

"Of course I care. Which is exactly why I need you to find someone else." The words caught in Joella's throat. She lowered her gaze. "How could I ever forgive myself if I let anything happen to her?"

"Help me understand here." Samuel pressed closer, his forearm resting on the table. "This can't still be about what happened to the child in Dallas. Is there something else I should know?"

She opened her mouth, ready to confess her fear of memory loss, but then found she couldn't force the words out, as if speaking them aloud would give them power. Foolish logic, of course, especially for someone who claimed to put her trust in God.

Instead, she opted for a half-truth. "Even after what you found out, I can't ignore my part in what happened to the little girl, and you shouldn't, either."

"Okay, call it an accidental oversight, slipup, mistake, whatever. You think I'm not going to make plenty of my own over Sophie's next eighteen years or so?" Jaw clenching, he looked away. "Only God knows how many mistakes I've already made in my lifetime."

The regret shading his tone crowded out her own concerns. She laid her hand on his. "If Scripture is to be believed, He's already forgotten."

"'For I will forgive their iniquity, and I will remember their sin no more.' Jeremiah, if memory serves." He slid a glance her way, and the tiniest smile curled his lips. "A timely reminder for both of us, don't you think?"

She could only nod.

"So," he began, sitting straighter, "will you please agree to continue watching Sophie in the afternoons?"

Her breath quickened as she weighed her

reply. *Lord, I want to, so much!* "All right," she said at last, "but only as long as you're nearby."

"If that's what it takes to restore your confidence." His lopsided grin threatened to undo her. "I'll even look in on you every hour. Every *half* hour if it'll make you feel better."

"No, no, that would only defeat the purpose. You need uninterrupted work time." She chewed her lip. "But maybe give me a call from time to time whenever you're between tasks?"

"And remember, you can always call me about anything." He pressed her hand as he stood. "I mean it—*anything*."

Five minutes after he left, she was still staring at the closed door and feeling the emptiness he'd left behind. *Don't you dare fall for him again*, her brain cautioned.

But her heart just wouldn't listen, apparently.

Chapter Seven

Life for Samuel began to settle into a comfortable routine. His mother continued watching Sophie in the mornings, and after lunch he'd take Sophie up to the apartment and wait for Joella's arrival. The first several times after their talk, he'd gone so far as to set two or three reminders on his phone each afternoon to either call or make an excuse to run upstairs for something. He told himself it was mainly to reassure Joella, but deep down, he had to admit the regular check-ins eased his mind as well.

Then things got busy as one bred mare after another went into labor. Samuel wouldn't be of much use in the foaling barn, so while his father and brother took charge there, he finished transferring years of ranch records to the new computer and generally reorganized the office.

With every horse's individual record in the

system, he was ready to enter data on each new foal as the mares delivered. They could now efficiently track growth, nutrition, immunizations and more. It sure beat trying to make sense of myriad scraps of paper stuffed into the dog-eared folders jamming the filing cabinet.

Around two thirty one afternoon, his father limped into the office on his crutches. "Two more, a filly and a colt. We almost lost the colt to a breech birth, but the vet got here in time."

"Which mares?" Samuel was already pulling up breeding records on the computer. As his father recited the details, his fingers flew over the keyboard. Typing—another skill he was proud of, and a high-school elective he'd never regretted taking.

Dad maneuvered around the desk to stand at Samuel's shoulder. "You got all that right there in the computer?"

"Yes, sir. And I can show you how to look up anything you need to know about any horse on the property."

"Humph. Fine, as long as we don't have a power failure or the computer doesn't blow up."

"No worries either way. The computer has a battery backup, and the data's also saved to the cloud."

Another harrumph, and Dad scanned the

ceiling as if searching for this mysterious cloud.

Samuel could only laugh to himself. "Seriously, there's so much more this program can help us with. Once we get through foaling season, I plan to start using it for pasture management. That way, we can track—"

"Hold on." Dad extended his arm, palm outward. "You want to tidy up the accounts with your fancy new software? Go ahead. But I've been working this ranch for most of my life, so I don't need a computer telling me how and where to graze my horses."

Samuel knew better than to argue. He should count it a win that Dad hadn't fought him any harder about migrating the ranch files to the new system.

His father left, saying he needed to get back to the foaling barn. Samuel only hoped his stubborn dad wasn't overdoing it.

He dealt with a couple of bills that had arrived in today's mail, then rubbed his bleary eyes and decided to take a break. At not quite two months old, Sophie was starting to notice her surroundings, and those early hints of a first smile never failed to spark joy in his deepest core. His baby girl might not get much out of visiting the new foals, but it was a pleasant early-spring day and Samuel couldn't resist the idea of taking her out to see them.

Upstairs, he found Joella rocking Sophie. Joella looked so relaxed and content that he could hardly take his eyes off her.

She beamed up at him. "She's been staying awake for longer and longer stretches, so we're having a little chat."

"I see. And what has my daughter been telling you about me?"

"Well, she said she loves you very much and hopes you'll give her a red Mustang convertible for her sixteenth birthday."

It was all he could do to keep from roaring with laughter and startling his precious baby. He leaned over her and wagged a finger. "Uh-uh, not happening, sweet thing. I may not even let you out of the house until you're thirty."

Joella snorted. "Overprotective much?" Then she winced. "Which you have every right to be."

He wasn't about to let her go off on that tangent again, not when they'd come so far in the past couple of weeks. "How about the three of us walk out to see the foals?"

"Really? That would be fun."

While Joella slipped on her sweater, he secured Sophie in the fancy strap-on baby carrier he'd picked up in town the other day. With his little bundle snuggled against his chest, they started out.

"Foaling season has kept me so busy that I haven't been much help with my grandfather's party. How's it going?"

"Humming along. I was over this morning to ask him and your mom a few more questions. Arturo was in good spirits, so we had a very productive conversation."

"Glad to hear it." Samuel snickered. "I know Tito can be a bit of a grouch sometimes."

Joella grew silent as they walked, a pensive frown turning down the corners of her mouth. "Have you considered it could be more than just being grouchy? You've said he's occasionally forgetful. I've noticed it, too. If he doesn't always recognize people he knows, or if he gets confused about where he is..."

Samuel bristled at the implications. "He's nearly ninety years old. Aren't memory problems normal at this age?"

"Somewhat. But certain types of memory lapses are more serious than others." She sighed. "Not sure if you're aware, but my mother died of Alzheimer's."

He halted in the middle of the lane. "Joella, I'm sorry. No, I didn't know."

She stopped a few paces away and turned, her head lowered. "I still have trouble talking about it. But it's made me hyperaware of anything resembling memory loss in other people."

Sophie squirmed and stretched, and Samuel rubbed her back while pondering what Joella had just told him. "Your mother had Alzheimer's? But she couldn't have been that old."

"Her diagnosis came exactly two months after her fifty-third birthday. She died two years ago, at age fifty-eight."

Dazed, Samuel shook his head. "I didn't know you could get Alzheimer's so young."

"It's called early-onset." Joella looked away, the grief in her expression a stab to his heart. "And yes, it happens more often than anyone wants to believe."

He covered the space between them and drew her into his arms, carefully so as not to crush Sophie. "I feel terrible for you, Joella. I had no idea."

"I still miss her so much," she murmured against his shoulder. "Most of all, I miss who she was before the disease began stealing her away. And I—" Abruptly, she pulled away, hugging herself as she inhaled deeply. "Anyway, I only brought it up out of concern for your grandfather."

"I'm glad you did. I'll talk to my parents about it tonight." Longing for the contentment he'd seen in her face while she'd held Sophie earlier, he sidled up next to her and linked his arm through hers. "In the meantime," he began, donning his most enticing grin, "milady did agree to accompany the little princess and her daddy to peek in on the newborn foals."

The beginnings of a smile crept across Joella's lips. "Oh, yes, I certainly did. Lead on, kind sir."

Walking arm in arm with Samuel, his sweet baby girl snuggled close, Joella wondered why it had to feel so natural, so right. She'd come to cherish her afternoons with Sophie more than she could express. If that weren't frightening enough, lately she'd also entertained dreams of a future with Samuel. Every moment she spent with him revealed deeper, more endearing aspects of the caring, responsible, godly man he'd become.

Why couldn't she simply accept their friendship for what it was and stop imagining the life she could never have?

After telling Samuel just now about her mother's Alzheimer's, she'd missed the perfect opportunity to reveal her private fear of developing the disease. But how could she, when their trust in each other—and more importantly, her trust in herself—had grown so much over the past several days? Things had been going too well to risk spoiling it all.

They'd arrived at the broad open doors of a modern-looking barn. Samuel nodded toward a small cluster of people watching something on the other side of a high window over one of the stalls. "We may have gotten here just in time. Ever seen a foal being born?"

"Never. You mean—" A thrill coursing through her, Joella sucked in a breath.

Samuel nudged her closer, then quietly asked the others if they'd mind making room so Joella could see.

Balanced on his crutches, Hank Navarro opened a spot at the front for Joella. Careful not to bump his injured leg, she smiled her thanks as she edged closer to the window.

In the stall, a dark brown mare lay on her side in a bed of straw, her belly swollen and her sides rising and falling with each breath. Two tiny hooves had just emerged, and in a matter of minutes the mare birthed a beautiful brown foal. After giving the mother time to begin licking and cleaning her newborn, a female stable hand wearing a ponytail slipped into the stall to tend to them. It wasn't long before the spindly-legged foal struggled to its feet and tottered about the stall, already nuzzling its mother for a chance to nurse.

Stepping away, Joella pressed a hand to her thudding heart. "That was…amazing."

Samuel lifted a finger to her cheek, brushing away a tear she hadn't realized had fallen. With a sad smile, he kissed the top of Sophie's head. "Makes me wish I could have been there to see my little girl come into the world."

The longing and regret in his expression brought an ache to Joella's throat. She slid her hand under his arm and gently touched her head to his shoulder. "I'm so sorry."

"Thank you. Let's go outside for some air." They wandered farther along the barn aisle toward the open doors at the other end, where a fresh spring breeze carried the scent of new grass. In a row of small paddocks, several mares grazed as their foals scampered and pranced around them.

Joella rested her forearms along a fence rail. "They grow so fast."

"No kidding. These little guys are gaining two or three pounds a day right now."

"I'm sure it's similar with calves. Only three of Audra and Lindsey's cows have given birth so far. I was too chicken to go out and watch, but after today I can't wait for the next one."

Sophie had fallen asleep, and Samuel adjusted her in the carrier. "Let me know when another calf is due and maybe I'll walk over with Sophie so we can all watch together."

"No!" The gruffly shouted word came from behind them. Arturo stood in the barn door, brows drawn together beneath his hat brim and an unreadable look darkening his stare.

"Tito, what's wrong?" One arm outstretched, Samuel moved toward him.

"You must never, *ever* take my Sarita to the McClement ranch." Arturo's voice shook with something between rage and fear. "Promise me!"

Hank Navarro appeared behind him. "Papi, it's okay." He patted his father's arm. "Let's go back to the house."

"Pero mi niñita—" Arturo's worried gaze was fixed on Sophie, and he didn't look as if he'd willingly leave her.

Thinking quickly, Joella grabbed Samuel's hand. "Let's all go to the house. I'm sure Sophie's going to be hungry soon, Mr. Navarro. You can rock her and feed her."

His expression softening, Arturo nodded. He reached out to stroke Sophie's cheek, and his face warmed into a smile. "*Sí, sí.* We must be ready with her bottle when she awakens."

Samuel's fingers closed around Joella's as he released a silent exhalation. "Thanks," he whispered as they followed his father and grandfather back through the barn. "I have no idea what that was about. I keep hoping he's getting past this feud business, but apparently not."

She hated to state what seemed so obvious to her—that Arturo's lingering bitterness toward the McClements might also be a sign of senility. If, mentally and emotionally, he remained stuck in the past, whatever happened all those years ago might seem as tangible to him as what he'd eaten for breakfast that morning.

It was going on five o'clock by the time they reached the house. Pulling Samuel aside, Joella told him she'd decided to head home. "I'll just run upstairs and get my things. Same time tomorrow for our morning run?"

"I'll be there." Samuel frowned, looking irresistible with a stray lock of dark hair falling across his forehead. "Thanks again for your quick thinking with Tito. It breaks my heart, but I'm beginning to believe you're right about him."

"I wish I weren't, but…admitting there's a problem is the first step toward knowing how to help." She mentally cringed. *Look who's talking!* "You'd better get inside and take care of your baby. I'll see you in the morning."

* * *

One of the nicest parts about jogging with Samuel was just being together without having to say much. It was hard to hold a meaningful conversation when both of them—or at least Joella, anyway—struggled for breath. She was growing stronger day by day, though, and it felt good.

Between afternoons with Sophie and preparing for Nora Nicolson's big sweet-sixteen bash the following weekend, Joella's days became a whirlwind of activity. This would easily be the largest function River Bend Events had hosted in the weeks since they'd been in business. With Audra's help, Holly had negotiated an arrangement with Audra's church to rent their commercial-grade kitchen facilities for food prep and storage. Lindsey, in charge of decorations, had boxes and bags piled high in the dining room. Spencer had mowed and marked off a swath along the driveway for parking. They'd hired off-duty restaurant staff from Bonnie's Bistro to assist with food service.

The pavilion was delivered on Friday, and to put a little more distance between party guests and cattle, Joella had it erected on the front lawn. With a buffer of live oaks and cedar trees and the DJ's speakers facing away from the

Navarro ranch, hopefully the sound wouldn't carry too much.

Before River Bend Events had officially opened, Arturo had tried to have them shut down, claiming concerns about the noise and traffic. But everyone knew it was really about the feud. Even now, when talking with Arturo about his own party, Joella carefully avoided mentioning the fact that her event planning business had any ties with the McClements. So far, he'd been either too enamored with Sophie or too excited about the gala to make the connection.

By the time the Nicolsons arrived Saturday afternoon, everything seemed in order. Joella had meticulously gone over her checklist at least twenty times that day alone. And even though the Nicolsons had provided the required proof of event liability insurance, Joella had phoned Mayor Nicolson only hours ago to double- and triple- and quadruple-check that no one on the guest list had any food allergies or other physical conditions that could be cause for concern.

"It all looks beautiful," Mayor Nicolson gushed. The buxom woman pumped Joella's arm as she gazed across the pavilion. Lindsey's table decorations sparkled beneath the twinkle lights draped from the tent supports. The DJ already had the latest hits blasting from the sound system, and several teens boogied on the portable dance floor.

"I hope Nora and her friends have a lovely time," Joella said. "And thank you so much for changing your mind and allowing us to host the party."

"After Samuel explained what really happened with that horrible tragedy in Dallas... well, let's just put it all behind us, shall we?"

If only it were that easy. Joella kept a smile on her face as she excused herself to check on Holly and her helpers, who were in the kitchen unpacking the food they'd brought over from the church.

On her way up the front porch steps, she met Lindsey coming out the door.

And she did not look happy. Fists planted against her hips, Lindsey demanded, "When were you planning on telling us?"

Gulping, Joella glanced around in search of what could have prompted such a question. Surely she hadn't overlooked something else from her past that could sabotage the success of their business. "I—I don't know what you're talking about, Linds."

"The email. From your former boss. Offering you your old job back."

Joella's stomach plummeted. "You saw that?"

Her friend had the decency to look momentarily apologetic. "Well, I couldn't help it. I was getting ready to print out the Nicolsons' final statement from your laptop, but your personal email account was still open, and I—" She crossed her arms. "I snooped, okay? I mean, when the subject line was staring me in the face, how could I not?"

Closing her eyes, Joella could still see it plainly: Please come back! More $$, more vacation time—say the word!

She pulled Lindsey toward the far end of the porch, where the music from the party tent wasn't so overpowering. "Yes, it's true. I was offered my old job back. Your snooping skills must be failing, or you'd have seen my reply. I said I've never been happier than since I moved to Gabriel Bend and partnered with my two best friends. I told her no amount of money or perks could convince me to return to the big-city rat race. Lindsey," she said, squeezing her friend's hands, "running River Bend Events with you and Holly is a dream come true, and I am *not* leaving. Okay?"

"Really, Jo-Jo?" Lindsey drew her into a quick hug. "I'm so, so sorry I read your email. Can you forgive me?"

"Of course. And I never meant to keep anything from you. Refusing the offer was a no-brainer, so after replying, I never gave it a second thought."

"I'm so relieved. I—" Lindsey sucked in a breath as her gaze shifted to someone on the other side of the porch rail. "How long have you been standing there?"

"Long enough."

Joella turned to see Samuel grinning up at them across the shrubbery. With a mock frown, she said, "Eavesdropping again? Honestly."

"It's hard not to eavesdrop when you accidentally come upon a conversation in progress." Smirking, he motioned toward the noisy party. "And you weren't exactly whispering."

At least the DJ was honoring their agreement about keeping the volume several decibels below "nuclear explosion" level. Still getting over her surprise at finding Samuel there, Joella hardly noticed when Lindsey patted her shoulder and then retreated inside the house. "And you came over because…"

"I was out back talking to my brother about Tito." Samuel came up the steps and joined her on the porch. "Do you have a minute? I don't want to bother you if you're busy."

She sensed his unease. "No, it's fine. I can keep an eye on the party from here."

"There was another incident this morning. Tito was calling Mom by my grandmother's name—Rosalinda. It was like he was back in the 1960s. He kept asking where she'd taken Enrique and Alicia, my dad and his sister."

"I'm so sorry, Samuel." Forcing a swallow, Joella lowered herself onto the porch swing. "Dementia is…difficult. For every member of the family."

Samuel joined her on the swing. "Mom and Dad want to have him examined by a doctor, but with his party only two weeks away, they're hoping seeing old friends will help ground him. Did it work that way at all with your mother?"

"It may have, if she'd allowed them to visit. But when she realized what was happening, she didn't want anyone to see her that way."

"That's too bad." He reached for her hand, weaving his fingers through hers. "It still hurts, doesn't it?"

"More than you know." Her words came out on a hushed breath.

Still holding her hand, Samuel set the swing in motion. The feel of his touch, combined with the gentle sway, helped to restore her composure.

After a few silent moments, Samuel nodded toward the party tent. “Everyone looks like they’re having a good time.”

“Yes, they do.” She smiled in his direction. “I can never thank you enough for saving us from losing this event. If we pull it off successfully, and then your grandfather’s party, too, both will go a long way toward establishing our reputation in the community.”

“And I’m glad to know you’ll be sticking around.” Withdrawing his hand, Samuel roughly cleared his throat. “For Lindsey’s sake, I mean. Spencer’s mentioned how much she’s counting on the event venue to make this ranch self-sustaining.”

“Yes, right. And Holly needs a steady income to support herself and Davey.” Joella’s fingertips felt cold in the absence of Samuel’s touch. She closed her fist and covered it with her other hand. “I should probably go check on...something.”

“Of course. Didn’t mean to keep you.” Samuel rose from the swing, then steadied it while Joella stood. “I need to get home to Sophie anyway.”

“Give her a kiss for me.” She smoothed the skirt of her mustard-yellow linen shirtwaist, only to notice Samuel gazing at her, and quite appreciatively, if she wasn’t mistaken.

He blinked several times, a quirky smile nudging up the corners of his mustache. "Sorry, it's just… I don't see you dressed up like this very often. You look lovely."

Warmth crept into her cheeks. "Thank you. I admit, I may have gotten a bit too comfortable with not having to wear office attire every day."

"Another good reason to stay in Gabriel Bend, right?"

Among so many others. "Excuse me. I think the mayor's signaling me over. Duty calls!"

Time to put some space between them before the hammering of her renegade heart betrayed her.

Chapter Eight

Over the next week, six more foals were born, and Samuel's father kept him busy entering details and updating growth charts. In between times, he educated himself on pasture management. Maybe once all the mares had delivered and they'd gotten past Tito's birthday gala, Dad would be more receptive to his ideas about making some changes.

On Monday morning, he'd just finished reading an article in the latest issue of *Western Horseman* when Spencer breezed into the office. "We have *got* to get you out from behind that desk," Spencer stated. "When was the last time you were on a horse?"

Laying aside the magazine, Samuel drew a hand down his face. "Uh…"

"Exactly what I thought. So go upstairs and

change into some *real* cowboy clothes, because I've already saddled a horse for you."

"Nice try, Spiny, but I don't have time for this." He flicked the mouse to wake up the computer and pretended to study something on the screen.

"Then you'd better make time, because I'm not taking no for an answer." Spencer reached across the desk and grabbed the mouse.

"Hey!"

Scooting out of reach, Spencer held the mouse over his head. "If you want this thing back, you've gotta earn it with a horseback ride."

"I am *so* going to get you for this, little brother."

"You're only two minutes older, so cool it. See you in the arena pronto, or this critter's going in the manure bin." Spencer marched out, slamming the door behind him.

Wow, could falling in love and marrying the girl of his dreams really have turned Samuel's usually reserved twin into this suddenly confident, smiling-all-the-time anomaly? And dare he admit he was a little bit envious? More and more lately, the time he spent with Joella sent his thoughts wandering through dangerous territory.

Groaning, he shoved away from the desk. He needed to get more work done, but he wasn't doing it without his computer mouse. Better to humor Spencer and get this over with. He only hoped his brother had had a talk with the horse about being patient and sweet-tempered with the out-of-practice city slicker.

Upstairs in the apartment, he changed into his scruffiest pair of jeans and tugged on the boots he hadn't worn in months. The equally seldom-worn black Stetson their parents had given him for Christmas hung on the coatrack, so he settled it low on his brow before heading down.

As he approached the arena gate, he found not just Spencer but also Lindsey and Joella waiting for him, all on horseback.

Spencer held the reins for a fourth horse and offered them to Samuel. "My rescues needed exercising, so I recruited a couple more assistants. This ol' boy's about your speed. His name's Trouble."

Samuel gingerly took the reins. The sleepy-looking sorrel looked harmless enough, but looks could be deceiving. "Should I be scared?"

"Only if you're worried about getting bored to death."

"Give it up, Samuel," Joella said, patting her horse's neck. "If I can do this, you certainly can."

This was ridiculous. He'd grown up around

horses, even did the 4-H thing as a kid. Just because he hadn't ridden much in the last several years didn't mean he'd forgotten everything he knew. With a surreptitious deep breath, he set his foot in the stirrup and hoisted himself into the saddle. As he settled, the horse did little more than twitch his ears and snort.

So far, so good. Mainly, Samuel didn't want to embarrass himself in front of Joella, who looked amazingly at ease on the gray she rode.

"A couple of times around the arena to make sure everybody's comfortable," Spencer instructed, "and then we'll head out for a trail ride."

Coincidentally—or not—Samuel found himself riding next to Joella. The brim of a baseball cap and a pair of aviator sunglasses obscured her eyes, but she was definitely grinning at him. "I never realized your brother could be so bossy," she said.

"Me, neither. Did he drag you away from your work, too?"

"He did. Not that I minded. I was going cross-eyed studying my checklists for your grandfather's party."

"Foaling season has kept me busier than I expected, but it's finally tapering off. Just let me know what I can do."

"We're ready to start decorating the barn

tomorrow. Holly and Spencer will be there, but Lindsey and Audra decided they'd better stay at the ranch on calf duty." Joella pursed her lips. "Also, they don't want to risk upsetting Arturo right before his party."

Samuel hated to admit it, but they were probably right. Tito'd had several good days this week, his spirits climbing as he anticipated his birthday and seeing all the old friends expected to attend. No reason to ruin his mood with unnecessary reminders about the feud.

Tito's reaction when Samuel had mentioned taking Sophie next door to see the calves had been worrisome enough. Since that day, the old man had grown even more possessive of the baby, and Samuel had urged his mother to be extra vigilant anytime Tito held her.

Spencer rode toward the arena gate. "Y'all ready to hit the trail?"

Soon they were back on the McClement ranch, with Spencer and Lindsey leading the way through a series of pasture gates and along the path to the river overlook. After a couple of early spring rains, the bluebonnets were beginning to carpet the fields with their vibrant blooms, and Samuel had to admit how much he'd missed the Hill Country's annual wildflower splendor.

Twisting in the saddle, Lindsey called over

her shoulder, "Joella, won't this be perfect for those engagement and bridal photo shoots we have scheduled over the next month?"

"Beautiful!" Joella shot her friend a quick smile. "That clearing we just passed with the big rock in the center would be a great spot."

Maybe he was reading more into her tone than was there, but Samuel couldn't help thinking she sounded wistful. Why did it seem as if she'd completely closed off her heart to any possibility of romance? Had he done that to her by hurting her so badly all those years ago? It pained him to imagine a gorgeous, talented, amazing woman like her giving up on love. If only she could someday see him as the kind of man she'd want to share her life with...

They'd reached the overlook, where the trail opened on an expansive view of a gently flowing arm of the San Gabriel River. Spencer dismounted and secured his horse to a tree limb, then helped each of them in turn do the same.

Joella wandered over to the edge of a short, rocky cliff. "This is where we used to have our kayak races, isn't it?"

"Right," Lindsey said. She pointed upstream. "That wide section of riverbank was our launch point."

Samuel came up beside Joella and gave her

a friendly jab with his elbow. "And as I recall, you usually won."

She grinned at him in a way that warmed his insides. "Anytime you want a rematch..."

"Do we even have the kayaks anymore?" Samuel looked toward his brother, who obviously wasn't listening since he and Lindsey had stepped away to share a tender kiss. A pang beneath Samuel's breastbone made him draw a quick breath.

Joella gazed at the newlyweds and sighed. "I think they've forgotten we're even here."

"Spencer deserves his happiness. Lindsey, too." Watching them, he added silently, *And so do we, Joella, if you'd give me a second chance.*

Just then, his cell phone chimed. He pulled it from his shirt pocket and glanced at the caller's name.

Toby Broski? Absolutely the *last* person on earth Samuel ever wanted to hear from again. Why would Chelsea's creepy ex-boyfriend possibly be calling Samuel? Whatever the reason, it couldn't be good.

With a glance at Joella, he turned away to answer. "What do you want, Toby?"

"C'mon. Is that any way to greet an old friend?" He used the same wheedling tone Samuel remembered.

"We were never *friends*." Samuel didn't know why he hadn't deleted Toby from his contacts months ago. "Get to the point."

Toby barked a harsh laugh. "You never were one to beat around the bush, even when you stole my girl."

"I didn't steal her. She dropped you because you didn't know how to play nice." Why was he even attempting to argue with this guy? "So again, what do you want?"

"All right, all right." Toby cleared his throat. "You remember Blair Merritt, the gorgeous redhead from the title company who always beat us at poker?"

"Yes, I remember." She was one of Chelsea's closest friends and her former roommate.

"Well..." Clearly enjoying this guessing game, Toby drew the word out for a full second. "She let it slip that Chelsea'd had a kid a couple months ago."

Warning bells clanged in Samuel's brain. He couldn't imagine where this was headed.

"So I started counting backward," Toby went on, "and I realized it had to have happened when you and Chelsea were fighting so bad. Guess you didn't know she came crawling back to me then."

The idea of Toby and Chelsea together made Samuel's stomach heave. "I don't believe it."

"Oh, yeah, believe it, my friend." Why did he have to sound so smug? "So I figured the kid could be mine. I heard Chels gave you custody and all, but naturally I want to do right by my own flesh and blood."

Samuel lowered the phone for a moment, his chest heaving with ragged breaths while he tried to process everything Broski was saying. *Dear God, don't let this be true!*

Joella clutched Samuel's arm, his distraught expression scaring her.

He returned the phone to his ear, his muted voice rough and full of rage. "Well, *you* can believe this, Broski. I'm not giving up Sophie without a fight, least of all to the likes of you."

Abruptly, he disconnected the call and clenched his fist. "This can't be happening. I won't let him near her."

"Who was that? What's going on?" Joella tightened her grip on his arm.

He looked past her toward Lindsey and Spencer, then to the horse he'd ridden. "I—I need to get back. I need… Sophie…"

"I'll go with you. Let's just—"

Spencer strode over. "You okay, Slam?"

"Not now." Already untying his horse, he waved his brother off and prepared to mount.

Lindsey captured Joella's wrist. "Wasn't Samuel just on his phone? Why is he so upset?"

"I—I'm not sure." She gave Lindsey's hand a squeeze. "Let me ride back with him and see if he'll talk to me."

Within seconds, she'd climbed into Ash's saddle and set off at a fast trot. She caught up with Samuel at the first gate. Riding side by side, neither spoke a word until they'd reached the McClement barn. Samuel made quick work of untacking his horse. After releasing it into a stall, he helped Joella with hers and then started across the field.

Keeping pace with his long strides, she was glad for the stamina those early-morning runs were building in her. "Just tell me," she said between breaths, "does Sophie's mother want her back?"

"No," he said, slowing as they reached the barbed-wire fence. Then, as if all the fight had gone out of him, he doubled over and planted his hands on his thighs. "Not Chelsea. But maybe...maybe Sophie's real father."

"But I thought—" She urged him to straighten and face her. "You mean you might *not* be?"

"I don't know anymore." His gaze darted as if it didn't know where to land. Then it locked firmly with hers. "I can't lose my daughter, Joella. I *can't*."

Her mind raced in search of some way to reassure him. "Your mom is watching Sophie, right? So go get her—*calmly*, so you don't get your mother all worried. We'll go up to your apartment and think this through."

He nodded. "Okay. Thanks." After helping her through the opening in the fence, he handed her his key ring. "Let yourself in. I'll get Sophie and be right there."

Watching for him from the living room window gave her a little more time to make sense of what he'd told her. Apparently, Chelsea hadn't been exclusive with Samuel while they were dating. Then how could she have been so sure the baby was his? Sweet little Sophie certainly resembled him, but without a DNA test…

The apartment door swung open. Samuel bustled in with his baby, who was fast asleep and snuggled against his shoulder. "Let me put her in her crib."

He started toward the bedroom but turned abruptly and brought Sophie to the recliner. He didn't have to explain. His desperate expression as he held his baby said it all.

While he cuddled and rocked Sophie, Joella sat close by on the sofa. Quietly, she asked, "You didn't have a paternity test to confirm?"

"It never seemed important. When Chelsea claimed Sophie was mine, I had no reason to doubt her word." He gave his head a grim shake. "Guess that sounds pretty stupid, considering the kind of people we both were at the time."

Joella didn't have an answer for that. After a moment, she said, "You realize there's really only one way to be sure."

"I know." Lips trembling, he traced one finger along Sophie's cheek.

He'd comforted and reassured Joella so many times over the past few weeks. Now she'd give anything to ease his torment. "The attorney who worked out your custody agreement—maybe he could help sort this out."

"Good idea. I should call him right now." He hesitated briefly before passing Sophie into Joella's arms.

She took over the rocker as he paced to the opposite side of the room to make the call.

He briefly explained the situation to the attorney, but he didn't look happy about what he was hearing in reply. "Okay, if that's the best you can do. Thank you."

"What did he say?" Joella asked as he lowered the phone.

"He can arrange for a paternity test, but it could be a couple of weeks before the Houston lab he deals with can work us in." He sucked in a breath. "Two weeks of wondering whether Sophie's mine or—or *his*. It'll kill me."

Joella chewed the inside of her lip. She could think of only one other person who could possibly ease his mind. Someone he should never have closed the door on. Softly, she said, "Maybe it's time you reached out to Sophie's mother."

He sighed and looked toward the window. "I can't. Mr. Schmidt repeatedly told me she didn't want any contact."

"That was a scared new mom talking. If she'd ever once held her baby—" An unexpected sob caught in Joella's throat. "She couldn't have had any idea what she was giving up."

Samuel dropped to his knee beside the chair and lightly rested his hand on Sophie's head. "I think she did know. I think she also knew herself well enough to do what was best for her baby."

"And she chose *you*, Samuel. Not this other man. Hold on to that."

"But if it turns out she's Toby's—" He shuddered and glanced away.

"So who is he? What do you know about him?"

"Toby Broski." Samuel spit the name. He pushed to his feet and resumed pacing. "Before Chelsea and I were together, she had a semi-serious relationship with him. He could be a mean drunk, and she broke it off when he started getting rough with her."

"How awful. How could she have gone back to him, then?"

"He's right about how much Chelsea and I were fighting around the time Sophie would have been conceived." He pressed his palms into his eye sockets. "If she was mad enough at me, it isn't a stretch to believe she'd go back to him out of spite."

"I'm so sorry, Samuel. But you could still be Sophie's father. Don't doubt it until you have proof."

"But if I have to wait two weeks? I don't know how I'll survive that long."

"Maybe you won't have to. I'm pretty sure you can get an over-the-counter test kit at the drugstore."

A spark of hope lit Samuel's dark eyes. "I've heard of those. But how fast are the results?"

"Here, take Sophie and I'll check online."

As he held his baby, she tugged her cell phone from her jeans pocket and opened her internet browser. A quick search brought up several results. She clicked on the top hit and scanned the page. "This one is available at most drugstores and should have a report available online within forty-eight hours of receiving your sample."

His hopeful look faded to a grimace. "No way I can pick up a paternity test at the local drugstore without everyone in Gabriel Bend knowing my business two hours later. My dad already thinks the worst of me. If word gets back to him that Sophie may not be his granddaughter, he'll never accept her, and he'll never forgive me."

Joella drummed her fingers on the chair arm. "I need to drive over to Round Rock on Wednesday to meet with the band who's playing for your grandfather's party. If you can stand waiting an extra couple of days, I'll buy the kit for you while I'm there."

"You'd do that for me?"

"Of course." She stood. "If you're going to be okay for a bit, I should get home and take care of a few things before I come over to babysit this afternoon."

"I'll be fine." He took her place in the rocker. "Actually, no need for you to come back. I think I'll spend the rest of the day with Sophie."

"All right, if you're sure." After taking the morning off for a horseback ride, she had plenty of work to catch up on, but she was worried about Samuel. Not to mention she couldn't help being a little disappointed. She brushed her fingertips across the baby's wispy brown hair, only a shade lighter than his. "And try to have faith. God must have had a plan when He brought Sophie into your life, so I refuse to believe He'd turn around and take her away."

"I pray you're right." He cast her a grateful smile. "Honestly, Joella, I don't know what I'd do without you."

"I'm glad I could help somehow." Straightening, she took a step toward the door, when more than anything she longed to stay, to offer whatever assurance Samuel needed right now. "I'll be over bright and early tomorrow with barn decorations, but I'll make sure I'm free by early afternoon. If you need anything before then…"

"I've got your number." The warmth in his gaze nearly undid her.

This would not do. She absolutely *could not* lose her heart and risk someday bringing even more pain into this good man's life.

Seconds after Joella walked inside, Lindsey and Spencer ambushed her in the kitchen.

"What did you find out?" Lindsey pressed.

Spencer spoke over her. "Is Samuel okay?"

Joella held up both hands, palms outward.

She'd anticipated this inquisition, so on the way home, she'd composed her response. "He's fine. The phone call was from some guy he knew in Houston who used to date Sophie's mother. He…he was saying some not-so-nice things, and Samuel got upset."

Lindsey folded her arms and harrumphed. "How tacky. And after he's worked so hard to turn his life around."

"Maybe I should go over there," Spencer said, starting for the door.

"Please don't." Snagging his arm, Joella shot him a pleading look. "He's calmed down now, having some quiet time with Sophie. I'm sure he'll be talking to you later."

Spencer gave a reluctant nod, retreating to share a quick kiss with Lindsey before donning his hat and excusing himself to do some work in the barn.

Lindsey hadn't given up so easily. She narrowed her eyes at Joella. "It's just you and me now. Want to tell me what's really going on?"

"I shouldn't. Just let it blow over, okay?" Her phone rang, saving her from having to say more. "It's the rental company. Probably confirming delivery for Arturo's party." Ducking around Lindsey, she headed for the study while pressing the answer button. "Hello, Joella James speaking."

While on the phone with the rental company rep, she saw Lindsey ride out with Audra, most likely to check on the cattle. That would keep her friend busy and hopefully forestall further questions for the time being.

With no need to return to Samuel's to watch Sophie, she spent the rest of the day working through her checklist for Arturo's gala. She'd had years of experience organizing much larger events than this, but at her previous company, she'd had access to whatever staff and equipment the occasion required. She had none of that here, though, and for a guest list the size of Arturo's, Holly couldn't possibly do all the cooking on her own. They'd once again arranged to rent the church kitchen for food prep beginning Thursday and had hired even more local restaurant workers to assist. The rental company would supply tables, chairs, steam tables, beverage stations and serving ware, in addition to the canopy, band stage and dance floor.

With her head about to explode, Joella shut down the computer a few minutes before five o'clock. After downing two ibuprofen caplets, she kicked off her sneakers and stretched out across her bed. Five more days and this party would be behind them. And not long afterward, Lord willing, Samuel would have confirmation that Sophie truly was his daughter.

Please, God, let it be so!

Please, Lord, let Sophie be mine!

Samuel lost count of how many times he'd repeated the prayer through a sleepless night. He knew his baby girl would rest more comfortably in her crib, but he couldn't keep himself from getting up frequently to check on her, sometimes standing over her for nearly an hour just watching her sleep. He loved the way her rosebud mouth worked, the way she'd sigh and raise her tiny brows, eyelids fluttering as if she followed the progression of a pleasant dream.

Dear Jesus, I know I've made mistakes, but I'm begging You...

Maybe Joella was right and he should try to reach Chelsea. If he could convince Mr. Schmidt to give him her contact information, he could call and ask her point-blank—*Is Sophie really my daughter?* He'd make her explain how she could ever have gone back to Toby, ask if there was anyone else while he'd thought they were exclusive. Yes, their relationship had been turbulent, but one thing he'd never done was cheat on her.

After Sophie's 4:00 a.m. feeding, he drifted off in the recliner with her nestled securely in his arms. Sometime later, with the first rays of dawn slanting through the window, he awoke to warm wetness seeping through his shirt. Great—he'd fallen asleep without changing Sophie's diaper.

As he stirred, she opened her eyes and blinked at him. He smiled and arched a brow. "Sorry about that, baby girl. Now we both need a change of clothes."

Within the hour, he'd cleaned up and given Sophie a bath, and they'd both had breakfast. Ready to head down to work, he decided at the last second to keep Sophie with him in the office instead of leaving her with Mom. He backtracked to grab her infant seat and diaper bag. When she needed her next bottle, he'd run up to the apartment and feed her there.

Not twenty minutes later, his mother barged into the office. "There you are! I've been waiting for you to bring Sophie over." Swinging her braid off her shoulder, she knelt in front of the infant seat and cooed at the baby. "Grammy missed you, sweetie. Is your daddy keeping you all to himself this morning?"

"Sorry, Mom. I should have let you know. I just…needed her with me." He couldn't tell her yet that the baby she'd grown so attached to might not really be her granddaughter. If the DNA test confirmed his worst fears, breaking the news to both his parents would be unbearably hard.

Mom offered an understanding smile as she came around the desk to give him a hug. "You're such a good dad. Have I told you lately how proud I am of you?"

Shame curdled in his gut. "Even with how I've messed up?"

"'Therefore if any man be in Christ,'" she quoted, smoothing the hair at his temple, "'he is a new creature: old things are passed away; behold, all things are become new.'"

One of his favorite verses from Second Corinthians. He patted her hand. "I've been leaning hard on that passage for a while now."

"Good. Keep it up." After dropping a quick kiss on Sophie's head, Mom moved toward the door. "Since you've got the baby, I can help Joella start fixing up the barn for your grandfather's party. When you get a break later, bring Sophie over and see how things are coming along."

"I will."

As the door closed behind her, he turned his attention to the notes the foreman had left on the desk late yesterday regarding the new foals. Time for more data entry. Truth be told, he was beginning to enjoy being a part of ranch operations. His family raised living, breathing creatures who had unique characteristics and were capable of responding to care and affection. Commercial real estate had been both challenging and lucrative, but he'd never exactly bonded with a steel-and-glass building or a vacant lot.

He reached a stopping point about the time Sophie began whimpering for another bottle. Gathering her into his arms, he took her upstairs to feed and change her, then buckled her into the sling and started across the ranch to the old barn.

Standing in the broad open door, he surveyed the progress. In addition to Mom, Joella, Spencer and Holly, it appeared they'd enlisted the aid of a few of the stable hands. Two were sweeping out stalls, and two more hauled in hay bales to place around the perimeter. Joella sorted through a plastic bin of decorations, while Spencer helped Holly affix large, colorful sombreros to the support posts between stalls.

"Looks good," he said, approaching Joella.

Holding a spool of wide yellow ribbon, she straightened and smiled. "How are you? You don't look like you got much sleep last night."

"Because I didn't." He cast an uneasy glance toward his mother on the other side of the barn.

"Will you still be able to pick up the, ah…*item* tomorrow?"

"Of course. I meant to tell you I won't be back early enough to watch Sophie for you, though."

"That's okay. We can manage. When do you think you'll get here?"

"Hopefully no later than three thirty or four. That should be early enough to package everything up and take it straight to the post office."

"Good. The sooner I know something…" The better he'd feel? Only if the results were in his favor. If they weren't, it didn't bear thinking about. He clenched his jaw. "Did Lindsey or Spencer ask you anything about yesterday?"

"They were concerned, naturally." She unwound several inches of ribbon. "I couldn't lie, so I told them a partial truth—that the call was from a guy from your past who'd said some ugly things and rattled you. I also said I was sure there was nothing to worry about."

He blew out a sharp breath. "I'm praying you're right about the last part."

Casting him an understanding smile, Joella lightly traced the swirl of hair on Sophie's crown. "She looks pretty cozy right now. If you're not in a hurry to get back, maybe you could help me make some bows."

"Uh, decorations aren't exactly my forte."

"Trust me, this'll be a snap." She showed him how to hold his index fingers several inches apart while she wove the ribbon through them. She tied the loops around the middle, then slipped them off his hands and spread the layers into a big, fluffy bow. "Ta-daa!"

"Wow, is there no limit to your talents?"

She laughed, and the sound made his heart lift. Being around her made everything look brighter. Even the air around them seemed to shimmer.

If this was what falling in love felt like, he wanted more of it, and he wanted it with Joclla.

Chapter Nine

Now that Samuel's dad was getting around better, his mother didn't mind watching Sophie for longer periods—a good thing in the final days leading up to Tito's party, because Joella had more than enough to keep her busy. Waiting for her to get back from Round Rock on Wednesday, Samuel found every way possible to distract himself, and it wasn't only because he was anxious about the paternity test. Helping Joella with the decorations yesterday had only deepened his growing feelings for her. Once he got past this thing with Toby Broski—once, God willing, he could rest easy that Sophie was his—maybe the time would be right to see if this thing between him and Joella could deepen into something more.

Two thirty rolled around, and then three o'clock. Unable to concentrate a moment longer on computer records or ranch management articles, he stood before the office window and stared toward the road. Finally, at three forty, Joella's car pulled into view. She climbed from behind the wheel, then reached back inside for her tote. Seeing him at the window, she gave a nonchalant wave and sauntered toward the barn. It was all he could do not to rush out, grab her by the arm and hurry upstairs to get this test underway.

Steadying himself with a deep breath, he stepped out the office door. "Hi. How'd your meeting with the band go?"

"Everything's on track." She nodded toward the house. "Is Sophie with your mom?"

"Go on up. I'll get her and be right back."

His next challenge was maintaining his cool while retrieving his daughter. Mom's first concern was Joella. "She's been running party errands all day. No need for her to watch Sophie. Just leave her here with me."

"It's okay. I'm done in the office for today." He lifted Sophie from the bassinet.

"But it looked like Joella was on her way upstairs to your apartment."

Despite his messed-up past, lying had never been part of his nature. Even so, he wasn't prepared to explain. He drew a slow breath through his nostrils. "Mom—"

The clank of crutches preceded his father's appearance in the doorway. For a fraction of a second, it almost seemed Dad had smiled at Sophie. His expression turned stony as he met Samuel's gaze. "Did you work on payroll like I asked?"

"Yes, sir. All handled."

Giving a single nod, Dad pivoted toward the den.

Mom patted Samuel's cheek. "He'll come around, honey. I meant to tell you, he actually rocked her for a few minutes this morning while I folded a batch of laundry."

"Really?" A pinprick of hope lit in Samuel's chest. All the more reason he had to prove Sophie was his.

"Go," she said. "You mustn't keep Joella waiting." Her knowing wink suggested she'd read something entirely different into Joella's visit.

If only...

When he arrived in the apartment, Joella already had the test kit laid out on the dining table.

"It looks pretty straightforward," she said, perusing the instructions. "First step is to go online to register the test and pay the lab fee."

Samuel eyed the materials. "And this will give accurate results?"

"That's what they claim."

While Joella held Sophie, Samuel opened his laptop and created an account with the testing company. Once he'd entered the necessary details along with his credit card information, he sat back with a huff. "Okay, let's do this."

After they collected cheek swabs from both Samuel and the baby, Joella sealed everything inside the mailer. "I'll drive into town and drop it off at the post office. It's going somewhere in Ohio, so they might not receive it before the weekend."

Samuel grimaced. "At least I have work and Tito's birthday bash to focus on."

"And by early next week, you'll know for certain that Sophie's yours." She spoke with more confidence than he could muster. She turned toward the door, then swiveled back, her lower lip caught between her teeth. "I was thinking, if you'd like some company tonight, I could order takeout from Bonnie's Bistro while I'm in town and we could have supper together."

He narrowed one eye and couldn't help smiling. "Kind of like...a date?"

"Yes—I mean, no!" Was she blushing? "I just thought we could talk or watch a movie to help get your mind off everything."

"I like that idea a lot. Thank you."

She looked momentarily stunned. “So… what should I order for you?”

“Surprise me.” As if he weren’t surprised enough already by her offer.

Warm anticipation spread through his chest. Yes, dinner with Joella could be a very welcome distraction. But much as he longed for things to be different, he’d better be careful not to push too soon for anything more.

Volunteering to spend the evening with Samuel probably wasn’t the smartest move Joella had ever made. *You’re playing with fire*, she reminded herself all through dinner. Afterward, when he let her rock Sophie and give her a bottle, she knew she was doomed. This was everything she’d ever wanted—the company of a good man, a baby in her arms, contentment rolling over her like wave after warm wave breaking gently upon the shore.

The next morning, she could scarcely recall anything they’d talked about, much less the plot of the movie they’d watched. And the fault was all her own. Instead of keeping her wits about her, she’d utterly disregarded the risk to her heart and had blissfully allowed herself to imagine a future with Samuel.

With Samuel and Sophie.

And three or four more children. Children

who looked a little like him and a little like her…

"Joella? Hey, Jo-Jo!"

Startled from her thoughts, she jerked her head up. "Holly. I didn't hear you come in. I was, uh…" *What was I doing?* Oh, yeah. "I was counting centerpieces."

"Really? Looked to me like you were staring into space." Holly set her purse on the entryway table and joined Joella in the dining room amid the boxes of party decorations. "You've seemed more than a little frazzled lately. Sure you're okay?"

"I'm fine. But Arturo's party is a hugely important event for us, and I don't want to overlook anything." She glanced at her checklist, then resumed her count—or rather, started over. "Eleven, twelve, thirteen…" She'd reserved twenty sixty-inch round tables, which could seat as many as two hundred guests. "I should check with Lois and see where the RSVPs stand. If we have to arrange extra seating, we'll need more table decorations—"

Holly silenced her with a light touch. "Stop obsessing. You've planned this out to the smallest detail. Everything's going to be perfect."

"Perfect?" Joella scoffed. "I have yet to pull off the *perfect* event. But I don't want to let anyone down, especially you and Lindsey."

"Or maybe yourself? Because if you're still trying to make up for what happened with the child in Dallas, it's already been determined that *wasn't* your fault."

"I know." She gave her head a quick shake. "You're right—I'm needlessly obsessing."

"So take a break and let's grab Lindsey for a cup of coffee before we haul all this stuff over to the barn."

Within the hour, they'd filled the bed of Spencer's truck with decorations and party supplies. Once everything was loaded, Joella and Holly climbed into the cab to ride over with Spencer. Again, Lindsey and Audra stayed home to avoid any unpleasantness with Arturo.

By the time they started unloading, Samuel joined them. Though he traded friendly gibes with his brother, Joella sensed his underlying tension. It wasn't hard to recognize, considering she carried plenty of her own.

Trying to lift a heavy box from the back of the truck, she stumbled. In a heroic feat of brawn and dexterity, Samuel grabbed the box while steadying her. "Easy, there. Where were you going with this?"

"Last stall on the right." She chose a lighter box and walked over with him. As they added their crates to the growing stack, she released a tired breath. "Thanks. The last few days before an event are always the most demanding."

An appreciative smile brightened his dark eyes, which were shadowed by lack of sleep. "I can't even imagine the brainpower required to plan and organize all this. You're pretty amazing, you know."

She looked away to hide the rush of heat in her cheeks.

Holly's timely arrival saved her. "There you are, Jo-Jo. Mr. Navarro is looking for you."

"Oh? I'd better go see what he needs." *And pray it's nothing major.* With a brisk nod to Samuel, she hurried off.

It turned out Hank wanted to confirm where the rental company would be setting up the portable restrooms. Satisfied they would be convenient but unobtrusive, he thanked her and left.

Samuel returned for another box. "Everything okay with my dad?"

"All taken care of." Joella consulted her planning notebook. "After we finish unloading the truck, can we take another look at the power connections?"

The day continued much the same as she checked off one detail after another and made sure they'd be ready for the rental delivery first thing in the morning. Tomorrow would be another hectic day arranging and decorating the stage, seating area and serving stations, while Holly and her crew continued food prep at the church kitchen.

As work drew to a close late that afternoon, she came upon Samuel outside the barn. With Sophie snuggled beneath his chin, he gazed toward the setting sun. Careful not to startle him, Joella softly called his name.

He drew a quick breath, as if drawn from some faraway place in his mind. "This time of day usually puts me in the mood for prayer. 'I will lift up mine eyes unto the hills, from whence cometh my help.'"

With a nod and a smile, she spoke the next verse. "'My help cometh from the Lord, Which made heaven and earth.' I love that psalm. It never fails to restore a measure of hope in me."

"Hope is what I need most right now." He kissed the top of his baby's head. "Sophie gave me her first real smile today. Mom claims she's already smiled for her, but I think she saved the best one for me."

"I'm sure you're right." Joella wouldn't mention she'd seen Sophie smile a few days ago. Recalling the moment still made her heart swell.

"I tried to snap a photo, but I didn't get my phone out in time."

"There'll be more. Lots more."

He cast Joella an anxious glance. "What if there aren't? What if the results prove—"

"Stop. Weren't we just talking about hope?" Facing him squarely, she gripped his arm. "Anyone with eyes can see Sophie's your daughter. Don't go borrowing trouble."

"I'm trying not to, trying to trust God, but I can't help worrying."

She understood that all too well. How long had she been fighting her private fears and striving to hold on to her faith? Releasing his arm, she swiveled away and hugged herself against an involuntary shiver.

"Joella?" Concern laced Samuel's tone.

"It's getting chilly. I should go find my sweater." She turned toward the barn, then paused to attempt an encouraging smile. "It'll be okay, Samuel. Somehow, it will be okay."

He really wanted to believe her. So why didn't she look like she believed it, too? Or was something else going on inside Joella's head? Too many times now, he'd gotten the clear sense that she held a part of herself locked away. The troubled look in her eyes moments ago seemed less about his predicament than about concerns much more personal to her.

Maybe it was only the stress of preparing for

Tito's birthday gala. Joella had certainly been consumed with working through her never-ending checklist. He'd lost count of how many times he'd seen her poring over the pages of her notebook as if some small detail could have changed in the last five minutes. Much as he admired her diligence, was she taking it to the extreme?

Sophie wriggled one of her arms free. When her tiny fingers brushed his beard, her brows drew together in rapt fascination.

"Don't you dare pull my whiskers, baby girl." His laughter elicited another of those precious smiles, and his heart melted all over again.

Treasuring such moments gave him the strength of will to close the door on his worries, at least temporarily, and concentrate on preparing for his grandfather's big celebration. Another distraction was the arrival of his aunt and uncle, Alicia and David Caldwell, and his cousin Mark, who'd flown down from Montana. Through Friday and most of Saturday, his mother and Aunt Alicia took turns watching Sophie so he could be available for whatever Joella needed help with.

By late Saturday afternoon, the old barn had never looked more festive—or less like a barn. Tito, attired in full *charro* regalia, roamed the space like an emperor surveying his domain. As guests began to arrive, he welcomed them with a sweep of his sombrero and a hearty laugh. Samuel couldn't remember when he'd seen his grandfather so ebullient.

The multitalented band Joella had hired alternated between mariachi and country-western music, with some pop and bluegrass thrown in. When they segued into a traditional Mexican waltz, Tito coaxed Samuel's mother to be his partner, his steps as smooth as a skater on ice as he guided her across the floor.

"They've both still got it," Spencer said, joining Samuel at his vantage point outside one of the beverage station stalls.

"Mom looks fantastic. Haven't seen her this decked out in ages." With her salt-and-pepper hair secured in an elegant French braid, she wore a bejeweled chambray dress that swirled about the tops of her lizard-skin boots.

"Where's Joella? You should get her out on the dance floor."

"I'm sure she's way too busy for dancing. Anyway, I've got my one and only dance partner right here." Samuel gave a nod to Sophie, tucked securely in his arms and wrapped in a cloud-soft pink blanket. "Why aren't you out there with Lindsey?"

"I would be, but she's still keeping a low

profile around Tito." Spencer scowled. "And she'd prefer to avoid Aunt Alicia, too, after what she found out a few months ago. Not that she blames Alicia, but it's still uncomfortable."

Spencer had confided what Lindsey had learned about her father and Alicia being in love as teenagers. Tito couldn't stomach the idea of his daughter marrying a McClement, so he'd sent Alicia to live with relatives up north. Lindsey's father had never gotten over losing her, and those buried resentments ultimately destroyed his eventual marriage to Lindsey's mother. Alicia, on the other hand, seemed to have found lasting happiness with Uncle David.

Samuel heaved a groan. "This feud business has gotten really old. I thought surely after Tito's heart attack, he'd finally put it behind him, but I guess it was too much to hope for."

The song ended, and after Mom thanked him with a hug, Tito resumed circulating among the guests. When his gaze landed on Samuel, his eyes lit up and he hurried over. "Ay, *qué bonita*—my beautiful little Sarita." He stroked Sophie's cheek. "I will take her now."

"Maybe later, Tito," Samuel said. "This is your birthday party. You should be mingling with your friends."

"Indeed, and I want to show off my baby girl." The old man held out his arms for Sophie. "*Dámela*—give her to me."

Something in his grandfather's expression made Samuel uneasy. "Okay, okay," he began, his tone placating. "You can hold Sophie, but how about you sit down first?"

"Good idea," Spencer chimed in. He hooked an arm around Tito's shoulder and guided him to his chair at the head table.

Relieved, Samuel followed close behind. Once his grandfather had taken a seat, he carefully placed the baby in his arms, then pulled an empty chair closer so he could keep an eye on things. Tito seemed a bit too wound up this evening to take any chances.

Within minutes, a parade of Tito's old friends began coming by the table. Tito's grin stretched wide as he basked in their congratulations and compliments on his precious great-granddaughter.

Except...he repeatedly called her Sarita, not Sophie. And he never referred to her as his great-grandchild but as "*mi hija*—my daughter."

Then, before Samuel realized what was happening, Tito shoved to his feet—still holding Sophie—and marched off in the direction of a latecomer. Dodging around the tables, Samuel rushed to catch up.

Tito greeted the elderly gentleman with a one-armed hug. "Claudio! *¿Cómo estás, amigo?*" He peeled aside Sophie's blanket. "Look at this beautiful baby girl Rosalinda has given me."

"*Sí*, Arturo, she is beautiful." Lips twitching in an awkward smile, the man cast Samuel a questioning glance.

Less concerned about the man's confusion than his daughter's safety, Samuel placed a steadying hand under his grandfather's elbow. "Tito, let me take Sophie. Please, I think you should—"

Jerking his arm free, Tito glared at Samuel, not a hint of recognition in his eyes. Before Samuel could gather his wits and figure out what to do next, he glimpsed Joella striding over, Spencer and Aunt Alicia right behind her.

Joella's narrowed gaze and tight smile said she'd witnessed this unnerving scene. "Arturo, I've been looking for you," she said brightly. "As the honoree, you need to say a few words, and then your guests have some stories to share."

Tito's brows drew together. He closed his eyes briefly as if trying to get his bearings. "I am to speak?"

Spencer came forward. "Yes, Tito, everyone's waiting."

With gentle insistence, Joella eased Sophie from his arms. "Go on up to the stage. I'll watch the baby for you."

Spencer and Alicia each took one of Tito's elbows to escort him. The music had fallen to a hush, and the drummer now beat a rousing cadence that seemed to compel Tito forward while at the same time quieting the crowd.

Heart thumping in a matching rhythm, Samuel breathed out a sigh of relief as Joella handed his daughter to him. "Thank you. I was about to panic."

"It's called redirection. I had to learn that with my mother whenever she got confused or anxious."

As he checked Sophie from head to toe to reassure himself she was unharmed, the baby encircled his thumb with her plump little hand, and the lavender scent of baby lotion calmed him. He looked toward the stage, where Spencer was helping Tito up the steps. "I had no idea my grandfather's dementia had gotten this bad."

"It can be scary, I know." Arms folded, Joella pressed her lips together.

With Tito's voice reverberating from the speakers, Samuel decided he needed a break from the party. "I'm going outside for some air. Do you have time to join me?"

Joella visibly relaxed. "Sounds wonderful. Can we get something to drink on the way? I'm parched."

At the beverage station nearest the main door, she picked up two bottles of sparkling water. They ambled out to an empty table at the far edge of the canopy and sat down facing away from the barn. The April evening was pleasantly warm, and nature's fragrance of wildflowers and meadow grass carried on the breeze.

Resting Sophie on his legs so he could gaze at her dimpled face, Samuel tucked the blanket around her. "I still haven't managed to capture one of her smiles with my camera."

"Do you have your phone with you? Let me try to snap a picture while you get her to smile."

"Great, thanks." He tugged his phone from the inner pocket of his blazer and handed it to her.

After setting down her water bottle, she took a position at his shoulder. "Okay, Daddy, start making faces or funny noises or something."

Who knew such silly sounds could come out of a grown man's mouth? But it was working. Sophie was soon "talking" to him, her big round eyes fixed on his facial contortions and her rose-petal lips bowing into the sweetest smile he'd ever seen. Click after click sounded next to his ear as Joella snapped photos.

"There, I'm pretty sure I got some good ones." As she handed him his phone, her fingers grazed his, and they both froze.

"Thank you," he murmured, their gazes locked. If he weren't holding Sophie just now, he'd have a hard time resisting the urge to kiss her. How could she not sense what he felt for her?

She abruptly broke eye contact and reached for her water bottle. "I should go see how the party's going. Maybe I can encourage your grandfather's friends to tell a few more stories to keep him entertained."

"Right. Let me know if—" But she'd already hurried away.

Shifting, he glimpsed Lindsey sitting alone a few tables away. When he caught her eye, she waved and came over. "Did Joella get some good pictures?"

"Haven't looked yet, but Sophie was sure smiling up a storm." He nodded toward the barn, where another of Tito's old friends had launched into a lively tale of their adventures competing in *charreadas*, the traditional Mexican rodeos. "You should be in there enjoying yourself. Get Spencer to dance with you later."

She tucked a loose strand of hair into her curly updo. "Maybe. I just don't want to cause a scene."

"Like Sophie and I haven't already?" Samuel scoffed.

"Arturo does love that baby," Lindsey said with a sad chuckle. "If only he'd stop remembering things that are better forgotten."

Spencer joined them and drew Lindsey into his arms for a kiss. "Sorry I abandoned you, honey. Things were getting a little tense with Tito."

"But you handled it well." She thumbed a bit of lipstick from the corner of his mouth.

Inside, the elderly *charro* ended his story and then Samuel's father took the microphone. After thanking everyone for their anecdotes and tributes, he invited the guests to join the serving line for the dinner buffet.

"I'm starved," Spencer said, taking Lindsey's hand. "How about we get in line?" He turned to Samuel. "Coming, bro? Or can we bring you a plate?"

"Y'all go ahead. It's almost time for Sophie's bottle."

He sat holding his baby for another few minutes and wished he could forget all about the looming question of paternity. But ignorance wasn't really bliss, and this weight wouldn't be off his shoulders until he had an answer. Even if he didn't get the answer he prayed for, the Acknowledgment of Paternity he'd signed meant he was still Sophie's father under the law, and he'd do everything in his power to make sure Toby Broski never came anywhere near her.

When Sophie began her usual fussing sounds that indicated hunger, he went to retrieve the diaper bag he'd stowed inside one of the stalls. As he emerged, an angry shout pierced the air.

"Stella McClement? How dare you set foot on Navarro land!" Tito's roar was unmistakable. "Is your husband not with you? Have the coward show his face!"

Stella McClement, Lindsey's grandmother? But she'd died years ago.

Samuel looked in the direction of the commotion, where a cluster of guests surrounding his grandfather edged away. In the center of the small circle stood Tito, his face contorted with rage. He pointed an accusing finger at someone—Lindsey! Spencer tried to shield her, while at the same time Mom and Aunt Alicia rushed to intervene. Dad wasn't far behind on his crutches.

"You know he is to blame!" Tito ranted, his face turning a deep shade of scarlet. "He killed her! Egan McClement killed my daughter!"

Chapter Ten

Joella had been assisting Holly and the food service team when she heard the shouting. Immediately, she looked for Samuel, hoping he and Sophie weren't in the middle of it. With the party guests forming a wall as they strained to see what was happening, she made her way around the perimeter.

She approached a woman she'd seen chatting with Arturo earlier. "What's going on?"

"Ah, the silly old man—he's still carrying on about the McClements." The silver-haired woman clucked her tongue. "His mind isn't what it used to be. He seems to think that young woman is Stella."

That young woman, Joella realized as the crowd parted enough for her to see, was Lindsey. She shoved her way closer while racking her brain for some way to defuse the situation.

By the time she made it past the onlookers, Hank and Alicia were leading Arturo in one direction, while Spencer drew a trembling Lindsey aside. Joella's first instinct was to go to her best friend, but as the event coordinator, she had a responsibility to reassure the guests.

She turned toward the stage, where the band had ceased playing in the middle of a song and looked as dumbfounded as everyone else. With determined steps, she marched onstage and commandeered a microphone. Mustering a placid smile, she said, "Ladies and gentlemen, if I could have your attention, please..."

After she'd repeated herself twice more, the hum of multiple conversations faded, everyone looking to her as if awaiting an explanation.

She only hoped she could give them one that would save what was left of the gala.

"Thank you for your patience. Reaching the grand old age of ninety is certainly worth celebrating, isn't it?" She paused for the anticipated murmurs of agreement. "Sadly, age isn't always kind. Many of you know Arturo has had some health concerns this year. He was so thrilled about seeing all of you tonight, but I'm afraid the excitement has taken a toll. He needs to take a break from the festivities, but I know he'd want you to stay and enjoy the music and the fabulous dinner our caterers have prepared."

She gestured toward the buffet line, and like confused but obedient sheep, the guests began to make their way over. With a quiet sigh, she returned the microphone to the lead singer and asked the band to continue playing. Her knees were shaking as she stepped off the stage.

Lois intercepted her with a quick hug. "I can't thank you enough, Joella. You knew exactly the right thing to do to calm things down."

"Just doing my job. How is Arturo?"

"Hank and Alicia walked him outside to try to settle him." Hand to her forehead, Lois exhaled sharply. "I have no idea what he was raving about—blaming Egan McClement for the death of his daughter? As far as any of us know, Alicia is Hank's only sister."

"With dementia, it's hard to know whether the memory is real or a distorted version of the past. It was the same with my mother as her Alzheimer's progressed."

"Yes, Samuel told us you'd been through something similar—I'm so sorry." Casting a worried look toward the side door, she murmured, "I hope this party wasn't a huge mistake."

Joella squeezed Lois's hand. "Once Arturo calms down, I'm sure everything will be fine."

"Praying you're right. I'd better go check on Lindsey. I feel awful for her." With a parting smile of gratitude, Lois hurried away.

A glance at the buffet tables assured Joella that Holly had everything under control. She hadn't seen Samuel recently. Had he witnessed his grandfather's outburst? Since most of his family remained preoccupied with Arturo, she needed to make sure he and Sophie were all right.

She found him pacing beneath the canopy outside the barn, the baby propped on one arm as he held her bottle while she drank. While Joella was still several steps away, he called out to her, "Is my grandfather okay? I couldn't do anything because of Sophie."

"Your dad and aunt are seeing to him. Spencer's with Lindsey." She nudged him toward a chair. "Don't worry about them. Sit down and take care of your baby."

"None of this makes any sense," he mumbled as he eased into the chair.

She repeated what she'd told his mother about distorted memories. "There's no way of predicting what will trigger an episode like this. Everything could seem perfectly fine, and then..." She broke off, images of her mother's worst moments bringing a catch to her throat.

Samuel cast her an understanding smile as he set Sophie's empty bottle on the table. Propping the baby on his shoulder for a burp, he released a pensive sigh. "I think Sophie may have been the trigger. You've seen how he is around her. I lost count of how many times this evening he introduced her as his daughter. And the way he always calls her Sarita—what if there really was another child that he's never spoken about?"

"But wouldn't your dad or your aunt have known?"

"You'd think so, but—"

"Samuel, I've been looking for you." Mark Caldwell, the twins' cousin from Montana, strode over. "Sorry to interrupt, but I, ah..." He cast Joella an uncertain glance. "I knew you'd want to know what's happening with Tito."

"It's okay." Samuel motioned his cousin to a chair. "Joella's a good friend."

Why did his choice of words have to hurt so much, when she'd determined friendship was all they'd ever have? Trying not to let her feelings show, she stepped to one side.

Mark plopped down, hands clasped between his knees. "Tito's still keyed up, rambling a lot, but what your dad and my mom are piecing together…it's pretty unbelievable. Seems all this has to do with the ultimate source of the Navarro-McClement feud."

It had happened during calving season, Mark continued explaining. Rosalinda, their grandmother, was six months pregnant at the time, and had walked over with young Hank and Alicia to see the calves. Though the cattle were behind a fence, a cow known to be aggressive and an overprotective mother charged the fence, startling Rosalinda. She fell hard, which caused her to go into premature labor.

"Our grandmother delivered a baby girl, who died at birth." Mark's mouth hardened. He looked straight at Samuel. "They named her Sarita, their little princess."

Joella gasped. Samuel dipped his chin.

"And Tito has blamed Egan McClement all these years for not getting rid of the cow the first time she showed aggression." Straightening, Mark slapped his hands against his thighs. "Seems with you having a new baby and Lindsey looking so much like her grandmother at that age, everything got mixed up in Tito's brain. We've all been wanting answers about the feud. Too bad it had to come out in such an ugly scene."

"But at least now you know," Joella said.

"With the truth out in the open, maybe everyone can finally let go of the past."

Frowning, Samuel absently patted Sophie's back. "Learning the truth and living with it can be two different things."

Mark stood. "I'd better check on my parents. Mom was pretty upset."

"Thanks for filling us in." Samuel gave a half smile and a weary wave as his cousin turned to go. His eyes fell shut, and he snuggled Sophie closer. No doubt his thoughts had returned to the one question he most needed an answer to.

"Samuel, it'll be okay." Joella wanted so badly to wrap him in her arms and reassure him. *I'm falling in love with you, Samuel, no matter how hard I've tried not to.*

But she couldn't. Not now, not ever. Arturo's episode tonight had been a brutal reminder of what Alzheimer's could do to a family. She'd already witnessed what her dad had gone through—the daily agony of watching Mom's decline, then the stress-induced heart attack that took his life only months later. Joella could never inflict such grief upon anyone she loved.

No matter how desperately she longed for things to be different, her relationship with

Samuel had to remain at a friendship level. *You owe it to Samuel. You owe it to yourself.*

Music from the band and the clatter of tableware recalled her to the present and her event coordinator duties. She rose and lightly touched Samuel's shoulder. "You've got your hands full with Sophie. Let me bring you a plate of food."

His eyes drifted open, and he smiled as he covered her hand with his. "Thanks, Jo-Jo. You're the best."

Her rebellious heart fluttered. "You haven't called me Jo-Jo since we were teenagers."

"Do you mind?" He looked suddenly worried he'd crossed a line.

"No, of course not. It's nice you think of me as a…a friend."

The slight change in his expression—from concerned to confused—told her it was time to end this conversation.

She stretched her mouth into a bright smile. "Be right back with your dinner."

While the party guests finished their meal, Samuel's father took the microphone to assure them Arturo was feeling much more himself and wanted to apologize profusely for the disturbance. "He's quite tired, though—it's been an eventful evening—so we thought it best for him to excuse himself early. He has asked me to convey his thanks for your attendance and for celebrating this special milestone with him."

Dad looked exhausted, too, from what Samuel could make out from this distance. He must have been even more stunned than Samuel to learn he'd lost an infant sister. Samuel hoped the guests wouldn't stay too much longer so the family could have some privacy as they dealt with the aftermath of Tito's revelation.

With Sophie napping on his shoulder, he'd managed to eat most of the meal Joella had brought him. Now all he wanted was to call it a night and tuck his baby into her crib. There'd be plenty of time tomorrow to catch up on whatever he'd missed.

The next morning, his mother texted to say his grandfather had had a rough night and they'd decided to skip church.

But join us for breakfast so we can all talk before Alicia, David and Mark leave to catch their flight, she'd added.

With Sophie fed and changed, Samuel carried her downstairs and walked over to the house. The rest of the family, except for Tito, sat around the kitchen table, a box of doughnuts and assorted pastries open in the center.

After such a busy week, Mom obviously hadn't felt up to cooking her usual Sunday-morning breakfast fare.

"Let me take that baby girl," Mom said, holding out her arms for Sophie. "Grab some coffee and have a seat."

He filled a mug and carried it to the table, where he pulled out a chair next to Spencer. "How's Lindsey?"

"She was pretty shook-up, but like the rest of us, she's relieved we finally have some answers."

Samuel shook his head and turned to his father, seated at the far end of the table with his injured leg propped on a footstool. "Dad, how did you not know about this?"

"As best I can figure, I was barely five years old at the time. Alicia was two. I don't think I even understood that Mama was expecting." He studied the bite of apple fritter on the end of his fork. "I do sort of remember walking over to see the McClements' calves, and something about Mama being startled by the cow and tripping on something. She was in the hospital for several days, and Papi left us with the McClements while he took care of her."

"I'm sure only because there was no one else close by to ask for help." Alicia wrapped her fingers around her coffee mug. "Even though

I was so much younger, I can still recall sitting on Stella's lap with her arms around me and feeling safe. It's the only real memory I have of being in her house, until…" She clamped her lips together and looked away.

Samuel exchanged a subtle glance with Spencer. Did Uncle David know Aunt Alicia had once been in love with Lindsey's father?

Dad knew, of course. He roughly cleared his throat. "After Mama was better, Papi broke off all ties with Egan. He said the McClements couldn't be trusted and that we must never go near them again."

Alicia quietly rose and poured the rest of her coffee down the drain. "We should finish packing. It's over an hour's drive to the airport."

"I'm all packed," Mark said. "We have a couple of hours yet. Anything I can do to help with cleanup?"

"That'd be great." Samuel swallowed his last bite of cruller and washed it down with a gulp of coffee. Leaving Sophie with his mother, he and Spencer and Mark headed out to the old barn.

Joella had stayed late last night helping Holly and the catering crew pack up the left-over food and serving equipment, so he was surprised to find them already in the barn boxing up decorations. As he made his way around the tables to where Joella worked, a tired but concerned smile lit her face. "How's your grandfather this morning?"

"Still sleeping. But Dad said he seemed much more lucid by the time they got him into bed last night."

"And you?" she asked, studying him. "Are you doing okay?"

Samuel helped her fit another centerpiece into a large plastic crate. "I'm still digesting the news. As is everyone in the family."

"It's got to be a relief, though. To finally know, I mean." The faraway look in her eyes hinted of something else lurking beneath her words. He felt more and more certain she carried an unspoken fear of her own.

And then it hit him—her guilt over missing the Dallas toddler's peanut allergy. Her over-the-top anxiety about getting everything perfect for Mayor Nicolson's daughter's party. And in the days leading up to Tito's birthday gala, the countless times he'd caught her checking and rechecking details he'd already seen her confirm.

Alzheimer's. Joella was terrified of developing the early-onset Alzheimer's that had taken her mother.

Gently, he removed her hand from the centerpiece she'd been fiddling with, his heart aching with the deepening love he felt for this woman. "Joella," he whispered, smoothing aside a strand of her silky golden hair, "you've been my anchor these past few weeks. Let me be there for you now."

She tilted her head to look up at him. "I—I don't—"

Gazing into her shimmering brown eyes, he wanted so badly to hold her in his arms. A quick glance around the barn told him the others were busy elsewhere, taking down twinkle lights, folding tablecloths, stacking tables and chairs. Confident no one was looking their way, he drew her into the shelter of his embrace. "You don't have to pretend with me. I know you're scared of getting sick like your mom."

When his lips brushed her temple, she softly sighed and nestled closer, tucking her head beneath his chin. "How did you know?"

He released a tenderly sardonic laugh. "How could I not have figured it out sooner?"

"Guess I wasn't hiding my worries as well as I thought."

"Why did you think you had to?"

"I don't know. Pride, maybe?" With a shudder, she pulled away and plucked on the yellow ribbon encircling a candleholder. "I didn't want anyone feeling sorry for me. Or worse, doubting I can do my job."

Samuel scoffed. "Seems like you're the only one doubting your capabilities."

"One mistake is all it takes. If it isn't overlooking a client's food allergy, it could be a faulty electrical connection, or a coffee urn set too close to the edge of the table, and someone's little girl accidentally bumps it and—"

"Stop." He clamped his hand on her arm and held it until she looked at him. "Just a few days ago, you were lecturing me about not borrowing trouble. That's actually scriptural, you know? So if God says it, maybe we should both try believing it."

"I know, I know. And I do try." Her lower lip trembled. "But what happened with your grandfather last night, what my mother went through—that could be me in ten or twenty years, and it terrifies me."

That did it. No way in the universe he could rein in his feelings a moment longer. "Joella... Jo-Jo...you're not alone. Let me in, okay? Because I'm falling hard for you. I didn't mean for it to happen—I thought I needed to get my own life in order first—but every minute I spend with you—"

"Hey, Slam!" Spencer's voice rang out across

the barn. "Can you give us a hand with these tables? Mark's gotta go soon."

Heaving a frustrated sigh, Samuel yelled, "Be right there!" He met Joella's confused gaze. "My brother may not be long for this earth. Don't go anywhere, okay? This conversation isn't over."

I'm falling hard for you, too, Samuel Navarro. And I never meant for it to happen, either.

Joella stared after him as he jogged across the barn. A minute more and he would have kissed her, and she'd have welcomed it. It was a blessing Spencer had interrupted them, because she desperately needed time to breathe before she jumped off this cliff.

Problem was, she was seriously considering taking that leap. If she did, it'd be pure free fall, with no chance of changing her mind.

Just Samuel's strong arms to catch her.

But was he thinking straight? Were either of them? Depending on the DNA results, his whole life could be upended—again. She'd support him either way, but she couldn't risk exposing her heart only to have it broken when he came to his senses. Because eventually he'd have to accept the futility of loving a woman with too many issues of her own and realize he'd only needed her as a friend and confidante during a difficult time.

She picked up another candleholder and found a spot for it in the crate. Cleaning up after the party was the only thing she needed to be thinking about right now. As for the future…

Lord, it's in Your hands. Help me trust You and leave it there.

By noon, the only remaining signs of last night's celebration were the pavilion and party furnishings the rental company would pick up first thing Monday morning. They loaded the crates of decorations and other supplies into the back of Spencer's truck, then trekked over to the McClement ranch to store everything in one of Audra's outbuildings.

As they finished, Joella could tell Samuel was angling for a way to be alone with her again. He lingered on the back porch until everyone else had gone inside. Stepping between her and the door, he cast her one of those boyish smiles that never failed to turn her insides to mush.

"Can we talk some more?" he murmured, urgency in those piercing brown eyes. Taking her hand, he wove his fingers through hers.

With physical and emotional exhaustion catching up with her, it would take so little for him to convince her they really could have a future together, but she couldn't lose her resolve. Heart thumping, she looked down at their linked hands. "I don't know if that's such a good idea."

"At least tell me I'm not wrong, that these feelings between us aren't totally one-sided."

"No, you're not wrong, but—" She slid her fingers from his, then massaged her knuckles. "I can't do this right now, Samuel. Please."

He lifted his hands in a conciliatory gesture before stuffing them into his jeans pockets. "Okay, I won't push. But I'm also not giving up." With a determined nod, he marched down the porch steps and headed across the field.

Oh, for a tiny measure of his confidence!

Shoulders drooping, she went inside, where Holly and Audra were setting out lunch fixings. With no energy for small talk, she made herself a ham-and-cheese sandwich and filled a tumbler with iced tea, then escaped upstairs to her room.

After a lengthy afternoon nap and then twelve hours of sound sleep overnight, Joella awoke Monday morning with a clearer head than she'd had in a long time. Three things she knew for certain. Number one, she'd committed to making River Bend Events a success, for her friends' sake as well as her own. Number two, she loved her work and she intended to continue doing it for as long as God allowed.

Number three, the feelings she had for Samuel were real and growing stronger every day.

What she didn't yet know was how—or if—she could ever act on those feelings. The best she could do for now was take one day at a time. And pray. Oh, yes, she'd be doing lots and lots of praying.

It was after ten o'clock by the time she ventured to the study. With several weeks before their next major event, she'd make the most of the downtime by updating the website and scheduling social media posts and ads to promote summer wedding reservations.

Lindsey sat at the desk, oversize reading glasses perched on her nose as she typed something into the ranch computer. She glanced up as Joella entered. "Hey, sleepyhead. I'll be finished in a minute. Just paying a couple of bills. And thanks to Audra's and my share of the River Bend Events profits, we'll actually have money left over."

"That's great, Linds. You worked so hard to make this happen."

"No, we all did. Did you see the latest online reviews? I was looking at them earlier. We're a hit!"

"What?" Joella had been so busy with Arturo's party that she hadn't checked their Yelp and Google reviews recently. She pulled out a chair at the worktable and opened her laptop. Scanning the reviews a few seconds later, she dropped her jaw.

Best event food ever—no rubber chicken from this caterer!

RBE is pure quality. Planning to use them for my next event.

Beautiful location, charming chapel. Couldn't have been happier with our choice for renewing our vows.

And from Mayor Nicolson: Joella James is a consummate professional. Our daughter's party ran smooth as glass.

"Wow." Joella pressed her fingertips to her temples. "This is wonderful. Amazing."

"Even better, we've already received three emails this morning from prospective clients asking for more information." Removing her glasses, Lindsey cast Joella a sincere smile. "I hope you and Holly will always be as happy with our partnership as I am, because outside of saving the ranch, nothing has meant more to me than doing this with you."

Tingling with relief and gratitude, Joella arched a brow. "Not even marrying your childhood sweetheart?"

"That goes without saying." Lindsey scoffed, then ducked her head as a pink tinge colored her cheeks. She glanced up, one eye narrowed. "Speaking of sweethearts… I couldn't help noticing the sparks between you and Samuel lately."

"Please, we're just good friends." Oh, those two pivotal words she'd come to loathe.

"*Good friends* don't hold hands and gaze into each other's eyes nonstop. Not to mention almost kiss." When Joella started to protest, Lindsey waved a finger in the air. "I saw you two in the barn yesterday, so don't even try to deny it."

"Okay, yes, we've had some close moments." Joella's breath quickened. "But things are—I mean, it isn't that simple. We both have reasons to be careful."

"Like what?"

Feeling cornered, Joella fidgeted with the hem of her pullover. "Oh, you know, past hurts and such…" Her phone chimed with an incoming text. *Saved by the bell.* "Excuse me. This could be one of those potential new clients."

Not a prospective client. Samuel. Results are ready. Can't look. Come over?

Keeping her expression impassive, she said to Lindsey, "I need to run next door. There's some…unfinished business to take care of."

"About Arturo's party?"

Joella gave a noncommittal wave and hurried out.

Five minutes later, she stood in Samuel's apartment as he paced in front of his laptop on the dining table. "The email must have come this morning while I was over at the barn meeting the rental company people. I wasn't expecting to hear back so soon, and now I—I can't—"

"It's okay. We'll do this together." She steered him to the table and urged him to sit. "I can look first, if you want."

He gave a shaky nod, his palms scraping up and down the legs of his jeans.

She sat next to him and shifted the laptop closer. The email from the DNA testing company was front and center, with a link to the online results. With a glance at Samuel, she clicked the link, which opened a log-in window. He gave her his passcode, and after a couple more security steps, the results page opened.

Abruptly turning away, Samuel hid his face in his hands. "What does it say?"

"I'm reading—hold on." She scanned slowly, not wanting to make a mistake. But as she read on, her heart sank. "Samuel, I'm sorry..."

Chapter Eleven

"Just tell me." Samuel straightened and hauled in a breath. He felt like he could throw up. "She's not mine, is she?"

"No. I mean—" Swiveling toward him, Joella clutched his hand. "It seems like there was some kind of technical problem at the lab. They couldn't complete the test."

He searched her face. "They couldn't—you mean there *aren't* any results?"

"That's what it says. There's a phone number to call if you want more details, but they say this is an extremely rare occurrence and they're going to refund your cost."

Like getting his money back would make up for the torturous last few days. Or help him survive the wait until the attorney could arrange for a legally valid test. This was a nightmare.

"Samuel, I'm so sorry. I should have done more research, found a more reputable company. If I'd only—"

"It isn't your fault, Joella." He pulled himself together enough to give her hand a reassuring squeeze. After all she'd done for him—all she meant to him—he wouldn't let her take the blame for some faceless entity's lab glitch. "No, this is all on me. It's the least I deserve for how badly I'd gone off the rails. Messing up my own life was bad enough, but my mistakes hurt Chelsea, too, and now a sweet baby girl—" Breaking off, he shoved up from the chair and stalked to the front windows.

"This isn't all your fault, either," Joella said, coming alongside him. "Chelsea was a consenting adult. She made choices just like you did."

"Without a single thought to the consequences."

Joella tucked her arm through his. "Sophie is a blessing, not a consequence."

His chin dropped to his chest. "A blessing I could lose."

"But you haven't lost her yet, and you still might not. Whatever the DNA results prove, you're the man Chelsea chose to raise her baby. As of right now, *you* are Sophie's only legal parent."

"On paper, anyway. But if it turns out she's Toby's—"

"She isn't." Leaning her head on his shoulder, Joella murmured, "A baby as sweet as Sophie couldn't possibly be the daughter of the jerk you told me this Toby Broski person is."

He choked out a pained laugh. "You're forgetting I used to be a jerk, too."

"Yes, but that's all behind you. I've seen how you've changed, what a good man you've become." Shifting to face him, she lifted her hand to his cheek, and he could have melted through the floor. "No one could ever be a better father to Sophie than you, and I'd do anything to help you keep her."

He covered her hand with his. "Sophie isn't the only blessing in my life. Joella..."

"Don't say anything more. Not now."

All he could do was nod and pray that *not now* meant *someday*, because with each passing moment his need to have her in his life intensified. Eyes closed, he kissed her hand, then lowered it to her side and stepped back. "You should probably go."

Her shaky smile said she understood. "Will you be all right?"

"I have to be. Like you said, for now, at least, I'm Sophie's only parent. I'll concentrate on staying strong for her."

Which was exactly what he did for the next several days. Around his family, he made a determined effort to hide his worries behind the easygoing confidence he'd always been known for. He even persuaded his dad to let him implement one of the pasture management methods he'd been reading about. The effectiveness wouldn't be evident for several months, but it was encouraging to know Dad had come to respect his ideas enough to let him try.

Then on Thursday morning, when Samuel took Sophie to the house before heading to the office, he found his father at the kitchen table with the morning paper and a mug of coffee. "Your mother had to run upstairs for something," he said gruffly. "Give the baby to me."

Samuel stared at him. "Are you sure?"

"You think I've forgotten how to hold a baby?" Dad laid the paper aside and moved his mug away from the edge of the table. Reaching for Sophie, he shot Samuel the glare he'd typically reserved for his wayward son's most serious infractions.

Even so, there was a hint of mischief behind the glare. Seeing it as a positive sign, Samuel laid Sophie in his father's arms. When she cooed and brushed her fingers across his chin, Dad chuckled and tenderly enclosed her tiny hand within his large one.

Samuel's eyes welled. He'd prayed for his father to accept Sophie. What if, after all this, they lost her?

"Son?" Concern laced Dad's tone.

"I, ah… I should get to work." Sniffing, Samuel backed toward the door.

"Not yet. Sit." His father motioned him toward a chair. With a deep sigh and his gaze locked on Sophie, he said, "I have been hard on you, I know. Perhaps even unfair."

"I get it, Dad. I had a lot to make up for. A lot to prove."

Lifting his eyes to meet Samuel's, Dad firmed his mouth. "No longer. In the time you've been home, you've given me every reason to be proud."

Samuel could barely speak over the lump in his throat. "Thanks, Dad."

"I don't speak those words to either of my sons often enough." He adjusted Sophie's blanket, then looked up with a hesitant frown. "I know you only agreed to help until my leg healed, but is there any chance…?"

He understood what his father was trying to ask, and he already knew the answer. He'd known it for a while now. "This is my home. I want to stay."

"Good…good. Because I would also like the

chance to watch this little one grow up and teach her about horses."

Chest aching, a desperate prayer in his heart, Samuel could only nod.

Later, as Samuel updated foal records in the computer database, Spencer stopped in. Dusting off his hat, he sprawled in one of the visitor chairs. "Don't you know staring at a screen all day is bad for your eyes?"

Another benefit of making his home at the ranch—bantering with his twin. "You risk your skull every time you get on a green broke horse. Worst case for me is needing reading glasses someday."

"Or getting carpal tunnel syndrome. Seriously, Slam, since when did you become a full-fledged desk jockey?"

He sat back and gave his brother a one-eyed stare. "Since Dad fell off a horse and *you* decided to get married and move next door to run your equine rescue program and take up cattle ranching with your new bride and her aunt."

Spencer's playful attitude faded. "Lately, every time I ride out with Lindsey or Audra to check on the new calves, I think of Lita getting scared by that cow and wonder about the baby she and Tito lost."

"I know. All these years and he never spoke

of it, just nursed his anger and let it ruin his health and his relationships." Samuel rose and came around the desk to take the chair next to Spencer.

"Secrets and lies," Spencer murmured. "Like with Aunt Alicia and Lindsey's dad. Nobody ever talked about that, either, and look at the damage it caused, both before and after the truth came out."

"I hate that Lindsey got caught in the middle of our family's issues."

"She's working on forgiving her dad for checking out on the family, but it was awkward for her, being around Alicia last weekend. And then Tito blowing up like he did..."

Samuel stretched out one leg. "He's been much more subdued this week. A couple of times when I've gone to the house to get Sophie at the end of the day, I've found him rocking her and staring into space. Then he just smiles sadly and hands her to me."

"Is he still calling her Sarita?"

"Not that I've heard. Mom told me she's peeked into his study a few times and caught him wiping his eyes as he looks through an old photo album. I hope this change means he's finally dealing with the past."

"After his heart attack, I'd hoped so, too. Lindsey found a picture of him and her grandfather back when they were best friends and ranching partners. When I showed it to him in the hospital, regret was written in every line of his face." Spencer blew out a long sigh. "I've been praying he won't take those regrets to his grave."

"Me, too." Samuel's cell phone rang. He reached across the desk to retrieve it, his gut tightening when he read attorney Jason Schmidt's name on the display. "Excuse me. I'll take this outside."

He pulled the office door closed behind him and took several steps down the barn aisle before answering. "Mr. Schmidt. I've been anxious to hear from you."

"I'm sure you have, so I'll get to the point. Mr. Broski has consented to a paternity test. If you can be in Houston with the baby tomorrow afternoon, the mobile lab tech will work all of you in over the noon hour and put a rush on the results."

"I'll be there. And no matter how this turns out, Chelsea gave Sophie to *me*, and I intend to fight for her."

Joella had just returned in the Mule utility vehicle with a young couple and their photographer after doing their engagement portraits at the river overlook. Telling them goodbye, she dropped them off at their cars, then parked the Mule in the equipment shed.

On her way to the house, she glimpsed Samuel jogging toward her across the field. His frantic wave drew her up short, and she changed direction to meet him. "What's wrong?"

"I just had a call from Mr. Schmidt." Breathing hard, he halted in front of her. "It's tomorrow, and I need you with me. Can you get away?"

It took her several seconds to put the pieces together. "You mean for the DNA test? Yes, of course."

His shoulders sagged as a relieved sigh escaped. "We'll have to get to Houston by noon. Will that work for you?"

"I'll be ready." She gripped his hands. "I know it'd be useless to tell you not to worry, but for your sake and for Sophie's, at least try. God's got this."

"Thanks." A hesitant smile creased his cheeks beneath his beard. "Just keep praying."

"Haven't stopped for a second."

His fingers caressed hers. "I should get back. When the call came in, I kind of left Spencer hanging."

"Go," she said, trying hard not to shiver at his touch. "I'll see you this afternoon at the usual time, and we can talk more about the plans for tomorrow."

"Right. In the meantime, I'd better think up some reason to give my parents for being in Houston all day."

"You haven't said anything to them yet?"

He glanced down. "I can't, especially not now, when my dad is finally accepting Sophie as his granddaughter."

"He is? Oh, Samuel, that's wonderful!" She pulled him close for a quick hug.

"He...he actually said he was proud of me." The catch in Samuel's voice made Joella's heart stutter. "He asked me to stay."

"Stay? You mean permanently?" Barely able to swallow, she studied his face. "What did you say?"

"I said yes. It was a long time coming, but this place finally feels like home." He cast a pensive smile toward the Navarro ranch. "It's where I want to be. It's where I plan to raise my daughter."

The determination in his tone made her long for such courage in herself. Courage to believe God really could turn the most devastating circumstances, even her own, into something hopeful, something good.

"Hey, is that a tear?" Samuel touched her cheek.

"It's nothing." Attempting a dismissive laugh, she retreated a step. "Didn't you say you needed to get back?"

He narrowed one eye. "This paternity stuff may have distracted me temporarily, but I haven't forgotten the conversation we never finished. One day soon, Joella, I promise, because you're another huge reason why I want to stick around."

She couldn't speak, only nod. Why did her heart have to tell her one thing while her brain insisted on itemizing all the arguments against it?

Later, when she went next door to take over Sophie's care, Samuel stayed only long enough to make sure she had everything she needed for the afternoon. Since he'd be taking tomorrow off, he wanted to get as much done ahead of time as he could. Returning upstairs at nearly five thirty, he apologized for keeping Joella so late. They decided on a time to leave in the morning, and Joella made him promise to try to get some sleep, even though she felt certain neither of them would have a restful night.

At five minutes before eight the next morning, Joella stood on the front porch with a small, soft-sided cooler of bottled water and snacks for the trip. At the last minute yesterday, she'd remembered to reschedule today's ten o'clock appointment with a couple interested in booking the chapel for an August wedding. Then she asked Holly and Lindsey to follow up with the Fritchells regarding arrangements for their family reunion. As preoccupied as she'd been with Samuel's situation, she prayed she hadn't let anything slip through the cracks.

It was easy enough explaining the trip to her friends. Samuel had some "loose ends" to tie up in Houston, and rather than impose on his busy mother for a full day of babysitting, he'd be taking Sophie with him and had asked Joella to come along to help. Naturally, her friends couldn't resist a few not-so-subtle gibes about her escaping for the day with her "beau."

Promptly at eight, Samuel drove up in his Lexus, braking at the foot of the porch steps. Joella darted down and climbed into the passenger seat. If the dark circles beneath Samuel's eyes were any indication, she'd been right about the sleepless night. She'd needed extra concealer to hide her own purple smudges.

She tilted her head to study him. "Are you alert enough to drive?"

"Are you kidding? I'm on a caffeine-and-adrenaline rush." He tipped his head toward the back seat. "Sophie, on the other hand, slept six solid hours between feedings last night. If necessary, I can let her drive."

It was good he could joke at a time like this. "Wonderful. Then I can feel safe dozing off for a bit." As he headed toward the road, she scooted deeper into the seat and closed her eyes.

Apparently, she really did catch a nap, because the next thing she knew, they were on Highway 290 just coming into Brenham.

"She lives!" Samuel teased, tossing a grin her way as she stirred. He had to be high on caffeine. Or else doing all kinds of mental gymnastics to distract himself from the purpose of this trip. "Want to stop for some Blue Bell ice cream?"

"Maybe another time." Hopefully when they had some good news to celebrate.

"We do need to take a break, though. Sophie's about to wake up hungry." He took the next exit and pulled into the parking area beside a travel center.

While he brought Sophie from her car seat, Joella unzipped her cooler and took out two bottles of water, offering one to Samuel. It seemed he took much more time than necessary to feed and change the baby, as if he weren't in such a hurry after all to get to Houston. As desperately as he needed to know the truth, every mile brought them closer to the possibility he wouldn't get the answer he hoped for.

Joella well understood the dichotomy—certain questions were better left unanswered. But not this one. Samuel would never find peace until he knew for certain Sophie was his.

By the time they reached the outskirts of the city, Samuel didn't need to make any extra effort to slow their progress—Houston traffic did it for him. Another forty minutes passed until he turned off I-635 and followed GPS directions to the attorney's office near the Galleria.

After shutting off the engine, he drummed his fingers on the steering wheel. "When I come face-to-face with Toby Broski, you might have to restrain me."

"I know you too well by now to believe that." She touched his arm. "Whatever happens in there, you'll be the better man. You'll *always* be the better man."

He met her gaze, his eyes seeking reassurance. "I hope you're right, because I can't lose my baby, Joella. Least of all to the likes of him."

"I *am* right." Joella willed confidence into

her voice while also sending up a silent prayer. She released her seat belt and grasped the door handle. "Let's go inside and get this done."

Mr. Schmidt's receptionist greeted them in the outer office. "Hello, Mr. Navarro. Please have a seat. Can I get you anything?"

"No, thanks, Helen." Samuel remembered the fifty-something brunette from when he'd met with the attorney to finalize the Acknowledgment of Paternity. Little did he know he'd be back here again so soon. He glanced around the empty waiting area. "Are we the first ones here?"

"Yes, sir. You're a little early, and Mr. Schmidt is currently meeting with another client."

Nestled in his arms, Sophie cooed at him. He jiggled her gently as he followed Joella to some chairs. Then he paused and returned to the marble reception counter. "So…how does this work, exactly?"

Helen cast him a patient smile. "The lab technician should be arriving shortly. Once the samples are taken, you're free to leave."

"That's…that's it? When do I get answers?"

Her smile never wavering, the receptionist replied, "It would be best if you hold your questions for Mr. Schmidt." She nodded again toward the seating area.

Feeling like he could jump out of his skin, Samuel paced to the windows, then back to where Joella waited. He wasn't aware of the bouncy amusement-park-style ride he was giving Sophie until Joella took hold of his arm.

"Either give her to me or sit down," she chided. "Or you might wish you'd brought a change of clothes for yourself."

Oh, yeah, he'd been introduced to baby spit-up firsthand more than once. Good thing Sophie'd had a couple of hours to digest her last meal.

At the sudden thought of Toby Broski taking over Sophie's care, Samuel practically fell into the chair next to Joella. Slumping forward, he could hardly grab a full breath.

Joella reached behind him and massaged between his shoulder blades. She didn't need to say anything. Her soothing touch was enough.

The outer door swung open. Samuel jerked his head up.

Toby.

It had been at least a year since Samuel had last seen him, and the creep looked pretty much the same. Flashy clothes that barely disguised a paunch, stubble darkening his jawline, and one of those trendy haircuts worn long on top and shaved close on the sides and nape of his neck.

Joella's hand crept over his, where he'd locked it around the armrest to keep from leaping out of the chair. He'd been smart to bring her along. Otherwise, he might be spending tonight in jail. *Time to be the better man Joella believes you are.*

Closing the door, Toby removed his mirrored sunglasses and scanned the room. He locked eyes with Samuel, and the corners of his mouth lifted in a twisted grin. "Hey, Navarro, long time no see." With a flick of his hand acknowledging the receptionist, he strode over and stopped in front of Samuel. He leaned sideways to look at Sophie. "Wow, what a cutie. Thanks for taking such good care of her for me."

Samuel's whole body shook with the effort to restrain himself. "Legally, I'm her father. You have a lot to prove before I'd ever give her up."

"Guess we'll see what the DNA results have to say about that. Unless..." Toby glanced over his shoulder and back at Samuel. He lowered his voice. "We should talk outside."

"Why?"

"Because maybe we can both leave here with what we want."

A typical Broski move, always looking for an angle. Rising, Samuel handed Sophie to Joella. "Take care of her, but come with me. I may need a witness."

Cradling Sophie, Joella shook her head. "This seems like a very bad idea."

"Exactly why I want you standing by." He helped her to her feet, then told the receptionist they were stepping out for some air.

Toby waited near a redbud tree just leafing out. He rubbed his palms together, his self-assured expression reminiscent of when they used to meet up for poker night.

Samuel halted three feet away. "All right, Toby. What's this about?"

Leering at Joella, who stood off to one side, Toby gave an appreciative smirk. "This your new lady? Kids can sure put the kibosh on romance, huh?"

"Which begs the question, why are you even here, Broski? Nobody ever mistook you for a family man."

"Listen, bro." Toby stepped closer and draped an arm around Samuel's shoulder like they were best buds. "I get that you're upset to find out Chels and I were making out behind your back. But it's nothing personal, okay?"

"Right. Nothing personal." Samuel struggled to hold his temper in check. He shrugged off Toby's arm.

A car circled the lot, pulling into a space near the Schmidt and Associates law office. A tall woman with close-cropped hair emerged carrying what looked like a medical bag.

"Samuel," Joella said, "we should go in. Sophie's getting hungry, and they'll need to take the swab before she eats."

Toby stepped in front of Samuel. "Look, we can end this right here, bro. I can see how attached you are to the kid, and the last thing I want is to cause you grief."

Yeah, sincerity was written all over the guy's face. "Spit it out, Broski. What *do* you want?"

"See, I was thinking..." He rubbed his palms together again, but this time it seemed less like confidence and more like frayed nerves. "When this DNA test proves I'm the kid's dad, everybody's lives get messed up. Most of all, the kid's. So I'm willing to drop the whole thing for, say, five grand. I mean it—five-K and I walk away. You'll never hear from me again."

Samuel looked at him askance. "That's your price for a child's future?"

"It's not like I'm selling you the kid. I'm just trying to do you a solid. You know, since you and your lady friend look like you're already playing house."

Rage flamed inside Samuel, and he knew it was all over his face, too. Making a fist, he drew his arm back, only to be stopped by Joella.

"He's not worth it," she stated, her gaze pleading. Holding Sophie against her shoulder, she cast a glance at Toby, then whispered, "He's nervous about something. I think you should call his bluff."

Pondering her words, Samuel eyed Toby while flexing his stiff fingers. She was right—this had to be a con job. An expensive one if Samuel fell for it and paid him off. And how long before the guy came back asking for more?

Heaving a dramatic sigh, he shook his head. "I can't do it, Toby. If Sophie's really yours, we all deserve to know. The lab tech's here, so let's do the paternity test and find out the truth." With a hand at Joella's back, he ushered her toward the law office and prayed he hadn't sacrificed his last hope of keeping his baby.

Chapter Twelve

A few steps from the office entrance, Toby grabbed Samuel's shoulder. "Not so fast, okay? You'd be making a big mistake."

Samuel spun around to face him, his index finger aimed straight at Toby's nose. "My first mistake—in the current situation, anyway—was ever giving credence to your claim to be Sophie's father. My second mistake was agreeing to meet you here."

"Fine. Fine!" Gaze shifting, Toby held up both hands. "You don't want to believe the kid's mine, that's your business. I can get a lawyer, too, and we'll fight this out in court." He turned in the other direction and jogged toward a rattletrap sedan with a dented fender. Seconds later, he peeled out of the parking lot.

Joella nudged Samuel's arm. "I really

thought he was bluffing, but...do you think he's serious?"

"If money's all he's after, maybe not. But he's a self-serving schemer, and I learned a long time ago not to put anything past him."

"Let's hope you never hear from him again. Here, want to hold your baby?" She shifted Sophie into his arms.

As he gazed at the perfect little bundle, Helen stepped out. "There you are. Mr. Schmidt and the lab tech are ready for you."

"Slight problem," Samuel said. "Mr. Broski apparently changed his mind about doing the test."

Looking confused, Helen scanned the parking lot. "In that case, let me find out what Mr. Schmidt wants to do next."

They followed her inside, and shortly the attorney signaled them into his office, where Samuel relayed what had happened out front. "He offered to forget the whole thing if I paid him five thousand dollars."

"An extortion attempt." Lips pursed, Schmidt shook his head.

"Knowing what I do about Toby Broski's gambling habit," Samuel said, cradling his baby, "it doesn't surprise me. But I'm still worried he might try something. Maybe even threaten or harass Chelsea. Is there anything you can do?"

"Unless he takes specific action, no. However, I will definitely let Ms. Walford know what happened today."

Old regrets twisted Samuel's gut. "You've spoken to her recently? How is she?"

"Doing her best to start over. That's all I can say."

Samuel nodded. His emotions had ricocheted all over the place today. He looked down at Sophie, and his heart melted anew. "So…we're done here?"

"I would strongly urge you to proceed with the paternity test." The lawyer tapped his pen on the open folder in front of him. "A result in your favor could forestall any further interference from Mr. Broski."

Joella sat forward. "I think you should, Samuel. You could settle any lingering doubts once and for all."

He was no longer certain he wanted to know. If it turned out Sophie wasn't his, even if he fought to keep her and won, could he bear the pain of knowing every day for the rest of his life that she was someone else's child?

And yet…for health reasons or otherwise, Sophie might someday need to know the truth. He owed it to her to find out.

Twenty minutes later, the lab tech secured the samples and related legal documentation in her bag. "Mr. Schmidt will have the report early next week."

"And I'll call you immediately upon receiving it." The attorney showed them out. Pausing at the outer door, he peeked around Samuel's shoulder to smile at Sophie. "Try not to worry, Samuel. No matter what the results prove, you are Sophie's legal parent until a judge rules otherwise. And it's obvious to me this baby couldn't have a more loving and devoted father than you."

"If you talk to Chelsea again, will you tell her how much I—" Samuel forced a swallow down his aching throat. "Tell her I said thank you."

On the way to the car, Joella linked her arm through his. He welcomed the support, because after the day he'd had, his knees felt like rubber.

Once he'd secured Sophie in her infant seat, he turned to lean against the closed door for a moment.

"Let me drive," Joella offered. "It's your turn for a nap."

He wouldn't argue. "But let's stop somewhere for something to eat before we head out of town. I'm starved, and Sophie needs her bottle, too."

Not far up Highway 290, Joella pulled off at an exit where they had burgers and fries from a fast-food place. With Sophie fed and changed, they were on the road again before two o'clock. Samuel reclined his seat and didn't know another thing until Joella nudged him awake in his own driveway.

He blinked several times. "We're home already?"

"You and Sophie both slept the whole way." Hands on the steering wheel, Joella wiggled her brows. "I, on the other hand, have decided to save my pennies for a Lexus. Sweetest car I've ever driven."

He decided not to tell her he was about ready to trade the luxury auto for something more practical and with fewer bad memories attached—not to mention lower monthly payments. Easing out of the car, he stretched his stiff muscles before opening the rear door to get Sophie. Just waking up, she greeted him with a smile that arrowed straight through his heart.

Joella came around the car as he lifted the baby out. "It's going to be okay. Everything's going to be okay."

Wanting desperately to believe it, he could only nod.

The back porch screen door swung open, and his mother called, "How was your trip?"

"Uh, fine," he said, fighting to control his emotions. "All good." *God willing.*

"Great. You're home in time for supper. Joella, will you join us?"

Please, Samuel mouthed. If he had any hope of keeping his composure around his family this evening, he'd need her calming presence all the more.

Her hand on his arm said she understood. Turning with a wave, she called, "Thanks, Lois. Count me in."

Could he love this woman any more than he already did? If only she'd allow herself to return his love. At times, she seemed on the verge of letting him in, but then the door would slam shut and he could sense her pulling away. Was she so afraid of losing her life to the same disease that took her mother that she'd given up on even the possibility of falling in love? As many times as she'd encouraged him not to lose faith, how could he convince her to do the same?

All through the meal, with her sitting beside him and chatting with his parents and grandfather as if she were already part of the family, he quietly admired her. Once, when Mom cast him an odd look and mentioned he seemed unusually quiet this evening, Joella jumped right in to say he was probably still groggy after his long nap on the ride home.

"Sleeping in the car always does that to me," she went on, then segued into a description of Houston's horrible traffic and how she wished they would have had time to stop in Brenham for Blue Bell ice cream. Since each member of the family had a favorite Blue Bell flavor, soon they were comparing and defending their personal choices.

Thanks to Joella's creative manipulation of the conversation, no one had an opportunity to press Samuel for details about their trip to Houston. He didn't think he'd be ready to talk about it until the final DNA results were in and he was certain there'd be no more dealings with Toby Broski.

Later, Joella helped Samuel's mother with the dishes, all the while going on about how she and Lindsey had finally convinced Audra to let them install a dishwasher. "With four of us living there now, Audra admitted she couldn't put it off any longer."

Mom snorted a laugh. "How she ever went this long without one is beyond me."

As they finished, Sophie began fussing, and

Samuel decided it was time to take her to the apartment and get her settled in for the night. It had been a long day for her, too, and though she'd fared pretty well, the sound of her cry indicated she'd hit her limit.

Scooping up her purse, Joella said, "I'll walk out with you."

He was hoping she'd say that.

With clear skies and only a sliver of moon glistening overhead, the stars shimmered like a million diamonds scattered across black velvet. Joella looked up with an audible sigh. "I may never get used to how many more stars you can see out here in the country."

"Amazing, isn't it? One more thing I've come to appreciate about moving home." His gaze drifted toward the darkened field on the other side of the fence. "Let me drive you. There's not enough light to find your way, and I don't want you tripping on something."

"I'll be fine. Besides, you need to get Sophie tucked in for the night."

Unable to disagree, he shifted the whimpering baby a little higher on his shoulder. "Let me grab you a flashlight, anyway. We keep several handy in the barn."

"Okay, if it's no trouble." She walked over with him.

He entered through the side door and flipped

a switch, illuminating the area of the barn nearest the office. Searching the supply cabinet one-handed, he chose a heavy-duty flashlight with a bright white front beam and a flashing red light in back. "This should get you home with no trouble."

Smirking, she took the light and swept it across the farthest reaches of the barn roof. "Perfect. They'll see me coming—and going—a mile away."

"I just want you to be safe." She might be joking, but he was serious. As serious as he'd ever been in his life. "Joella, I care about you… so much…"

Her smile faded. Her huge brown eyes glimmered as the flashlight's red light blinked steadily.

Sophie's restless cries became more insistent, but he couldn't let Joella leave yet, not until she understood exactly how much she meant to him. One hand caressing the baby's back, the other supporting her bottom, he bounced her gently. "Don't go home yet. Please. Give me ten minutes to get Sophie settled down."

Joella wasn't sure why she'd agreed to go upstairs with Samuel—she should have gone straight home—but now here she sat, rocking and soothing a fussy baby while he warmed a bottle of formula.

She was only helping him out, that was all. It couldn't be anything more.

He joined her in the sitting area. "Want to feed her?"

"Wouldn't you rather—"

He took a seat on the sofa and handed her the bottle, leaving her no choice. Over the past few weeks, she'd come to love holding and caring for Sophie, so why, tonight, did she suddenly feel trapped?

When the baby wriggled onto her back, eyes fixed on the bottle, tiny fingers grasping air and her heart-shaped lips working, something shifted in Joella's chest. *Dear God, I want this so badly! To be a mother...a wife...*

She glanced over to find Samuel gazing at her, his tender smile leaving no doubt as to his feelings.

For his daughter, yes. But also for her.

When are you going to stop avoiding the truth, Joella? He's in love with you. And you're in love with him. So what are you going to do about it?

What *could* she do, when the very real possibility remained that she could someday lose her memory—her *self*—to a cruel and unrelenting disease?

Stifling a shuddering sigh, she returned her attention to the baby, who sipped contentedly while seeming to study her with eyes as fathomless as the deepest part of the river. "What are you thinking, little one?"

"She's thinking what a great mom you'd be," Samuel murmured, "and how much she'd love to be held by you every single day, exactly like this." He shifted close enough to run his fingers along her arm. His voice roughened. "And I'm thinking how much I'd love to sit here watching you hold my baby—*our* babies. Every single day. Exactly like this."

Warmth spread through Joella's limbs. She tried to swallow, but her throat had closed. "Samuel, I told you why I can't."

"Can't? Or won't?" He knelt beside her, his gaze pleading. "I know what you're afraid of, Jo-Jo, and I'm as guilty as you of being scared of what tomorrow could bring. Aren't you the one who keeps telling me not to give up hope?"

"Yes, but—"

He released a soft laugh. "I wasn't asleep the whole time in the car this afternoon. I did some thinking, too. And I realized nobody but God knows what tomorrow will hold. Each day is a gift, and I'm pretty sure God doesn't want our worries about what may or may not happen in the unforeseen future to keep us from savoring every moment of the life He's given us today."

Joella nodded mutely as a tear slid down her cheek. Sophie had finished the formula, and now her eyes fluttered closed. Taking the bottle, Samuel set it on the end table, then pushed to his feet. He lifted Sophie into his arms, and with a firm glance at Joella that communicated *don't leave*, he carried the baby to her nursery.

He had no idea what he was asking of her, no idea what loving her could mean for his future, for Sophie's. A wife who might someday not even recognize her own husband? Even worse, whose memory lapses could endanger his child?

No matter how much she loved them both, she couldn't allow him to coax her into a choice that could ultimately bring only heartache. Soundlessly, she gathered her things and slipped out.

She was almost to the fence when she realized she hadn't brought the flashlight. Pitch blackness enshrouded the gap where they usually crossed between the separated strands of barbed wire. No telling what nocturnal critters lurked in the brush. It'd be safer to take the long way around the road, but she'd have to hurry because any minute now, Samuel would notice she'd left. Hopefully he wouldn't try to catch her, since it would mean leaving Sophie alone upstairs.

A dim yard light helped her pick her way along the driveway, but once she moved beyond its glow and reached the paved road, she felt as if she'd stepped inside a long black tunnel. Creeping along in the dark, she wanted to run but didn't dare, or else risk a misstep and topple into the ditch. The last thing she needed was a sprained ankle or broken arm.

When her cell phone chimed from inside her purse, she nearly jumped out of her skin. Of course it would be Samuel. She almost didn't answer, but then decided he deserved some kind of explanation.

"Hi," she said, grateful for the muted glow from her phone screen. "I'm sorry for running out, but I could tell where the conversation was going, and I… I'm just not ready."

He didn't speak right away. "You forgot the flashlight."

"I know." Cringing, she squeezed her eyes shut. But only for a moment in case anything sinister might be lying in wait. "Clearly a huge mistake."

"So why aren't you using the light on your cell phone?"

Duh. Maybe she really was losing her mental faculties. "How do you know I'm not?"

"Because I've been watching from the window and I would have seen it. At least you took the road instead of crossing the field."

"I do have a few working brain cells left." Did she sound as snippy to him as she did to her own ears?

He sighed. "Jo-Jo..."

"I'm really tired, okay?" Palm to her forehead, she strove for a gentler tone. "I don't think very well when I'm tired. And I need—"

What, exactly?

Clarity. Hope. A measure of assurance that dreams really could come true.

More silence from Samuel, along with another frustrated sigh. She pictured him combing his fingers through his hair. "Be careful getting home. And turn on your cell phone light."

Did he think she'd forget—again? And yet his tender concern deepened her feelings for him even more. She wished she could say the words aloud—*I love you, Samuel Navarro.*

She lowered the phone and pressed the disconnect button, then selected the flashlight feature. The beam wasn't very strong, illuminating only a foot or two ahead, but it kept her securely on the pavement until she turned up the McClement driveway and could rely on Audra's front porch light.

After climbing the steps, she turned with relief and gazed in the direction she'd come. Everything beyond the reach of the porch light was swallowed in darkness, but she'd made it safe and sound. And all she'd needed was enough light for the next step.

A nagging voice told her there was a message in this, a reminder that she didn't have to see the whole picture in order to move forward. A little faith could take her a long way.

All the way into Samuel's arms and as many years of loving him as God allowed?

If only…if only.

On Saturday, Joella didn't have much time for philosophical thoughts about her future. Two different photo shoots were scheduled at the ranch, one for a couple's engagement portraits and the other for five high-school classmates getting their senior pictures done. Lindsey took charge of the engaged couple, leaving Joella to corral the teenagers, three of whom insisted on being photographed in a field of bluebonnets with one of Audra's adorable white-faced calves. To ensure everyone's safety, Joella asked Audra to be on hand for those shots.

Returning to the house with Lindsey after seeing their clients off, Joella glimpsed Samuel out for a walk with Sophie. He paused and waved to her across the field. She offered a tentative wave in return before hurrying inside.

Lindsey caught up with her in the kitchen. "Yesterday you spent the entire day with Samuel, and today you barely acknowledge him. Did y'all have a fight or something?"

"Of course not. It's been an exhausting day, that's all." Taking a glass from the cupboard, Joella filled it with ice water and then gulped it down. "Next time *you* get to handle the senior photos. I forgot how wildly spontaneous teenagers can be. One of them actually asked if he could have his picture taken *riding* a cow."

"Give me a break. As I recall, you were the *wildly spontaneous* member of our threesome." Lindsey filled a glass for herself before plopping down at the table.

"I've matured since then." Legs aching from hours of clomping through rough pastureland, Joella sank into a chair.

"It's more than that." Lindsey pursed her lips. "You're…different somehow. I sensed it when we were first talking on the phone about going into business together, and since you've been here, it's even more obvious. Tell me, Jo-Jo. Is something wrong?"

Samuel already knew what held her back. Now it was time to be fully honest with her best friend. Long past time, if she were honest with herself. Nudging her water glass aside, she massaged her temple. "Ever since my mother was diagnosed with Alzheimer's, I've lived in fear that it's genetic and I'm destined to get it, too."

"Oh, honey, why didn't you say anything?" Lindsey scooted her chair around to clutch Joella's hands. "I knew your mom's illness hit you hard, and then losing your dad so soon after your mom passed away. But I never realized—" Her brows shot up. "This is why you haven't let yourself get close to Samuel? Because you're afraid of getting Alzheimer's?"

Joella nodded. "What Mom's illness did to my dad—I'd never want to burden Samuel that way. Especially now that he has a little girl to raise."

"But you know he wouldn't see it like that. You've got to tell him."

"Actually, he figured it out for himself the day after Arturo's party."

"And?"

"And you're right—he's been nothing but supportive. Last night—" Joella sniffed back a tear. "Last night he made it clear how much he cares for me, how much he'd love for us to have a future together."

Lindsey gasped. "He proposed?"

"Not in so many words. But I couldn't let it go that far, so I left."

"Joella!" Disappointment rang in Lindsey's tone.

"I know, I know. I've been praying so hard about this, and I keep hoping with time..." With a despairing shrug, she gave Lindsey's hand a squeeze.

Lindsey squeezed back. "Well, you can count on plenty of prayer from me. And if it's okay with you, I'd like to share what you've told me with Holly and Audra. Spencer, too. We can all be praying."

Throat aching, Joella nodded. Why had she ever thought she could do this alone, when she could have had her friends' prayers and reassurance, could have been upheld by their unwavering support?

It struck her suddenly that her parents had made a similar mistake. When her mother had started forgetting things, as a respected businesswoman she'd been humiliated and tried her best to hide the truth about her disease. When disguising her symptoms became impossible, she'd taken early retirement and soon became a recluse. Joella would willingly have requested a leave of absence from her job to help care for her mother, but her parents had refused all outside assistance until nearly the end when Dad had reached the limits of his strength. Ultimately, the combination of Alzheimer's and prideful self-reliance had robbed her of both her parents.

Was this really how she wanted to live her own life—shutting out the people she loved most due to the false belief she was protecting them? Her parents' choices certainly hadn't protected her, instead leaving her with not only grief but underlying resentment at being denied the chance to lovingly care for the woman who'd raised her.

Returning her thoughts to the present, she rose tiredly and bent to give Lindsey a hug. "Thanks for being such a great friend. I don't know what I'd ever do without you."

"And don't plan on ever finding out," Lindsey replied gruffly. "I mean it. BFF—best friends forever, remember?"

Tears threatening, Joella tightened her embrace. "No matter what happens, promise me that's one thing you will *never* let me forget."

Chapter Thirteen

Five days since Samuel had taken the paternity test at Mr. Schmidt's office. Five days since he'd shared his heart with Joella. How much longer could he stand waiting for the two *yeses* he yearned for more than anything he'd ever wanted in his life? Joella still came over every afternoon to babysit Sophie, but during his promised regular check-in calls and a few in-person visits upstairs, she'd made it clear she wasn't ready to talk. He worried about her—worried she'd attempted to carry this burden alone for too long. If she'd only let him in. If she could only trust God with her future—*their* future—and give love a chance.

The only good news was that he hadn't heard anything more from Toby Broski. He hoped the guy wasn't lurking in the shadows ready to press a paternity suit or thinking up some other way to cause trouble—either for Samuel or Chelsea. As tempestuous as their relationship had been, he worried about her, too. Her sacrificial decision to give up Sophie couldn't have been an easy one. She deserved the freedom to rebuild her life, and Samuel prayed every day that the Lord would open her heart and show her a better way.

Glancing up from the computer screen on Wednesday morning, he glimpsed his father and brother talking outside.

Hands on hips, head down, Spencer wore a grim expression. Balanced on his crutches, Dad clapped Spencer on the shoulder, and they both headed toward the barn.

Moments later, the office door swung open.

"Can you spare a few minutes?" Dad asked, working his way over to a chair. He'd gotten his cast off a few days ago but wasn't allowed to put his full weight on the leg yet.

Samuel looked between his father and his twin. "This looks serious. What's up?"

"It's your grandfather," Dad said. "His mind is going a little more every day. He wanted to help your mother feed Sophie this morning, but instead of putting the bottle in the warmer, he tried to use the stove."

Samuel's gut tensed. If there'd been a fire—"Is everyone okay?"

"Your mother discovered it in time, thank the Lord. But if he'd turned the burner on, I hate to think what could have happened."

Spencer palmed his Stetson as he leaned against the door. "Joella's been through this. We should talk to her."

"Please," his father urged. "We have to make some decisions soon, and if Joella can offer suggestions—"

"Not sure that's such a good idea." The last thing Joella needed was more evidence of dementia's effects on a family. "Anyway, we're not talking much these days."

Spencer cast him a pointed stare. "You're going to give up on her so easily? You need to talk to her. And I don't mean just about Tito."

"Don't you think I've tried?" Samuel swiveled his chair to face the side wall. "She's scared, and if I push too hard, I'll only drive her further away."

"If you ask me, you're not pushing hard enough. She's on the edge, Slam. Which way do you want her to fall?"

No question about that.

"Go over there right now," Spencer insisted. "Don't put it off one minute more."

So now Samuel's horse-whispering twin was a relationship expert? Guess he thought he'd learned a thing or two during his roller-coaster romance with Lindsey.

"I don't know," Samuel said, pulling a hand down his beard. "How do I even begin?"

His father snorted. "You can start by not being as stiff-necked as your old man. I almost lost your mother, you know. Her father didn't think a Latino horse breeder was good enough for her. If I hadn't swallowed my injured pride and fought for her, well…you two wouldn't be here to have this conversation."

Samuel had heard the story before. It surprised him, though, that Dad was even aware of his feelings for Joella. "Fine," he said tiredly, pushing up from the chair. "I'll see if she'll talk to me."

Five minutes later, he stood on the back porch next door while trying to work up the nerve to knock.

When he finally did, Lindsey answered with a sympathetic smile. "Hi. Spencer texted to say you were on your way over. Joella's expecting you. She's in the living room."

"Uh…okay." He'd half expected she'd refuse to see him.

Lindsey stepped past him onto the porch. "I'll be in the barn doing some chores, and no one else is home, so you won't be disturbed."

Insides jumping, he hauled in a breath and

strode through the kitchen, his sneakers barely making a sound on the wood floor. Peeking into the living room, he found Joella watching him from the sofa, a nervous smile twitching across her lips.

"Hi," he said, sidling into the room.

"Hi." The fingers of her right hand lifted an inch or two off the sofa cushion in a hesitant wave. "Come sit down. I know why you're here."

How could she, when he wasn't entirely sure himself? He lowered onto the edge of the chair closest to her. "Spencer thought you might—but if it's still too hard—" Great. Once again, he was as tongue-tied as his twin used to be.

"It's okay, Samuel. I know I've kept my distance since the other night, but I've had a lot of praying and soul-searching to do."

"I've been trying to give you space."

"I appreciate it. And I want you to know I'm thinking much more clearly about…so many things."

He cleared his throat. "That's good. I think."

"It *is* good. And long overdue." She shifted, drawing one leg under the other so she could face him. "So, about your grandfather. What your family is facing is so hard, and there are no one-size-fits-all answers. Any advice I could offer can only come from my personal experience."

"Of course."

"Then here it is." Lifting her chin slightly, she met his gaze. "Treasure the moments you have, and don't face the hard times alone."

In the thoughtful silence that followed, he studied her. "Sounds like good counsel in any situation."

"It does, doesn't it?" She glanced down, then up again. "I learned it from someone who's come to mean a great deal to me."

Warmth spread through his chest. His voice roughened. "Anyone I know?"

"You can probably guess. Oh, and one more thing—a valuable lesson gleaned from forgetting a flashlight on a dark night. You don't need to see the whole path in order to take the next step."

"More good advice." He hoped he wasn't reading more into her words than she'd intended. "Does this mean—"

Of all the times for his cell phone to ring! With an exasperated groan, he tugged it from his pocket. Then, seeing Jason Schmidt's name on the display, he sucked in a breath. "This could be the results."

While the phone continued ringing, Joella scooted closer. "Samuel, you have to answer."

Eyes filled with conviction, she wrapped her fingers around his arm. "Whatever he says, it's going to be okay. You and Sophie will both be okay."

He gave a quick nod, and with shaky fingers, he answered, then pressed the speakerphone button so Joella could hear. "Hello? Mr. Schmidt?"

"Good morning, Samuel. I have the results you've been waiting for." The man's professional tone gave nothing away. "Is this a convenient time to talk?"

Convenient? What did convenience matter when Sophie's identity was at stake? He clutched Joella's hand. "Please, just tell me."

"The DNA results confirm indisputably that you are Sophie's biological father. Obviously, this invalidates Mr. Broski's claim, so you shouldn't expect to be bothered by him again."

He let out a whoop. The phone fell to the carpet as he swept Joella into his arms, both of them laughing and crying at the same time as they clung to each other.

"Hello?" Schmidt's voice came from somewhere beneath the ottoman. "Samuel, are you still there?"

Catching his breath, he released Joella and dropped to his knees, fumbling for the phone. "I'm here. Sorry." He drew the back of his hand across his damp cheeks. "I'm so relieved. Thank you!"

The attorney chuckled. "Glad to be the bearer of good news for a change. I also wanted you to know," he continued in a more serious vein, "I've spoken again with Chelsea and conveyed your message to her. She asked me to tell you she's more certain than ever that she made the right choice in giving Sophie to you. She reasserted her promise never to interfere, as well as her hopes that if Sophie should someday want to meet the woman who gave birth to her, you wouldn't automatically say no."

"Of course not, as long as it's in Sophie's best interests. Chelsea will always be her mother."

"She'll be very grateful to hear that, I'm sure. In the next few days you'll receive a copy of the DNA report by certified mail. Now I'll let you get back to celebrating. All the best, Samuel, to you and the lovely lady in your life."

The call disconnected, and Samuel dropped the phone onto the ottoman. He reached for Joella and drew her close as a grin played across his lips. "Can I give the 'lovely lady in my life' another hug?"

"I'd like that," she said with a shy smile.

He enfolded her in a tender embrace. "And… ah…" This was turning out to be a pretty good day, so why not take another big risk? "Would the lady mind if I kissed her?"

She tilted her head, her tone softening. "I think I'd like that, too."

No way was he giving her time to change her mind. With one hand cradling her head, the other pressed against the small of her back, he lowered his lips to hers. He wished he could hold her in his arms forever.

"Tell me this is really happening," he whispered against her cheek. "Or if I'm dreaming, don't wake me up."

"It's true," she murmured. "Sophie is really yours."

He drew his head back far enough to shoot her an arched-brow look. "I didn't just mean the part about being Sophie's dad."

She tucked her head against his shoulder. "I know. And you didn't dream the kiss, either."

His heart felt like it could pound out of his chest. "Does this mean you're willing to give us a chance?"

"I… I want to—I really do." She peered up at him, a scared but hopeful glint in her eyes. "Maybe if you kiss me again…"

"Happy to oblige."

* * *

Joella wasn't naive enough to believe one kiss—or rather, more like three or four by the time Samuel headed home—would instantly erase everything that stood in their way. The Navarros still had difficult decisions to make concerning Arturo's long-term care. And the possibility of Joella's developing Alzheimer's would always linger in the back of her mind.

The possibility, she kept reminding herself. Not the certainty.

She'd told Samuel how much she wanted to give their love a chance, and in those moments of feeling so safe and secure in his arms, she'd meant it. It was time at last to put aside her questions and doubts, to live in the moment and let God show the way forward. With His help, she intended to try.

The next morning, work took priority as she was quickly immersed in plans for the Fritchell family's upcoming reunion. Holly had arrived a half hour ago, and Lindsey joined them in the study.

"...and Mrs. Fritchell changed her mind and requested sushi," Holly was saying, "so I'll be picking up some eel and octopus—"

"What?" Jaw dropping, Joella gaped at her friend.

Holly cast her an enigmatic smile. "Just making sure you were listening."

Which she clearly hadn't been. She consulted her notes. "So ribs and brisket, then. As originally planned. Everything still on track with renting the church kitchen for prep?"

With the memory of Samuel's kisses lingering upon her lips, she fought to keep her head in the discussion while they reviewed a few more details. They were just wrapping up when her phone pinged with an incoming text from Samuel. Missing you since yesterday. Dinner tonight at my place, 6-ish? I cook a mean frozen lasagna! And take the afternoon off from Sophie duty. I'm overdue for some major housecleaning!

The message ended with a smiley face and five heart emojis.

She gave a soft laugh, which naturally piqued Holly's and Lindsey's attention. Without giving them the satisfaction of an explanation, she texted back: Sounds great! Let me bring a salad and dessert. And don't go to extra trouble on my account! I've seen your apartment, remember?

She tacked on a wink emoji, and after a breath-holding pause, she added a couple hearts of her own.

"Wow," Lindsey remarked as Joella pressed

the send button. "I haven't seen you wearing a smile like that since…" She gave her brows a meaningful wiggle. "Hmm, since you visited the ranch with me the summer before our senior year in high school."

Holly's eyes widened. "Is it true—you and Samuel—*finally*?"

"Yes—maybe—" Feeling her face redden, Joella shrugged. "Let's just say things are moving in a positive direction."

"Oh, honey, I'm so glad!" Holly popped up from her chair and came around the worktable to give Joella a hug. "Ever since Lindsey told me about what was holding you back, I've been praying."

"Thanks. And please don't stop, because I'm not all the way there yet, and I'm still so scared."

Audra had just stepped into the room. She *tsk*-ed. "Show me anyone who's ever been in love who *hasn't* been scared at some point. I was terrified every time Charles deployed. What if he didn't make it home this time? Or what if—" Her voice broke.

Lindsey stretched an arm around her aunt's waist and gave her an encouraging smile while she composed herself.

"If I'd known what the future held, would I have changed anything?" Audra continued, her eyes brimming. "Not on your life. I count every minute I had with Charles a blessing—even during his recovery, when there were days he didn't want to go on living and I was terrified of losing him to the darkness. But we had each other, and we had our faith, and we learned that love is so much more powerful than fear."

Throat clenching, Joella plucked two tissues from the box on the windowsill, handing one to Audra and using the other to dab her own cheeks. If she could talk to her dad right now, would he tell her the same thing? Of course he would. He and Mom were as devoted to each other as any couple Joella had ever known. Their misguided insistence on privacy and independence aside, it was why Dad had given up everything to be Mom's caregiver during the last years of her life.

You know Samuel would do the same for you. As she would for him, if the tables were turned. That was how love worked. And buoyed by the support of friends and family, they'd never have to carry on alone.

After one more quick swipe, she crumpled the tissue and tossed it in the trash can. "Have we covered everything we needed to about the reunion?"

Holly and Lindsey, looking teary-eyed themselves, exchanged glances.

"I have all the information I need for now," Holly said.

"Me, too," Lindsey agreed.

"And I should get back to my calves." With a knowing smile and a wiggle of her fingers, Audra backed out of the study.

"Okay, then." Joella stood and closed her laptop. "I have some errands to run. See y'all later."

She made a quick trip upstairs to grab her purse and keys, then jumped in the car and headed into town. First stop, Bonnie's Bistro, where she placed a take-out order for a large Caesar salad with dressing on the side and one of Bonnie's acclaimed pecan pies. While the food was being prepared, she browsed the shops along Central Avenue.

A baby-blue satin poet blouse in the window of Janeé Clare's caught her eye, and she went inside to try it on. The flowing drape and tiny fabric-covered buttons made her feel like a princess. With skinny jeans and sparkly sandals, it would be the perfect combination of elegance and casual for tonight's dinner.

Janeé, the boutique owner, complimented her excellent taste as she rang up the purchase. "Special occasion?"

"I'm hoping it will be." After handing Janeé her charge card, she perused the contents of the glass display case beneath the register.

Her breath hitched as one particular object brought a rush of memories. "How much is that?" she asked, pointing.

"It's lovely, isn't it? Handmade by one of our local artisans." Janeé opened the rear of the case and bent to check the price tag.

Joella tried not to gasp at the amount the woman quoted. Still, it was perfect—exactly what she needed to complete her plans for tonight—and she couldn't resist. "I'll take it."

Pulse skittering and a bounce in her step, Joella made a few more stops before returning to the bistro to pick up her order. One final item had yet to be found among the belongings she'd brought with her to Gabriel Bend, and she only hoped she hadn't misplaced it.

Lasagna in the oven, soft music on the stereo, the table set for two with Mom's china and silver atop a lace tablecloth…

Candles. He should have thought of candles.

Releasing a frustrated groan, Samuel stared at his reflection in the bathroom mirror. Was he trying too hard to create the perfect romantic evening? *Slow down, Navarro, or you'll scare the lady off for good.*

With Joella expected any minute, it was a little late to redo the table setting. Maybe he'd forget the navy herringbone tie he'd planned to wear with his light yellow dress shirt. Better go easy on the cologne, too. Yeah, he'd gone way overboard with his plans for tonight. Blame the surge of hope yesterday's kisses had sparked.

At the same moment a knock sounded on the apartment door, Sophie awoke from her nap with a whimper. He'd debated accepting Mom's offer to babysit, but decided the deepening bond between Joella and the baby could help tip the scales in his favor.

"Come on, sweet thing," he murmured, lifting Sophie from her crib. "I'm counting on you to be your daddy's daughter and help me lay on the ol' Navarro charm."

Tucking the baby against his chest, he went to the door.

One look at Joella and he completely lost his power to speak. She'd done something different with her hair, clipping it up in back and leaving a few honey-gold spirals to frame her face. The stylish blue blouse brought out the highlights in her hair and made her brown eyes shimmer.

"Um, you're staring."

"Right. It's just…you look amazing."

"Thank you. So do you." Grinning, she held

out a Bonnie's Bistro bag. "Looks like you have your hands full. Shall I put this in the kitchen?"

"Sure." He opened the door wider and motioned her inside. "The lasagna should be out of the oven in another ten minutes or so. Sophie just woke up and I was about to feed her."

Joella set a plastic container of salad in the fridge, then spun around. "Oh, can I do it? I missed spending the afternoon with her."

His plan was already working. "That'd be great. Want to hold her while I get the bottle ready?" Before handing Sophie over, he whispered in the baby's ear, "You know what to do, sweetie."

Joella narrowed one eye as she snuggled Sophie against her shoulder. "What did you just say to her?"

"Nothing. Just told her to be a good girl for you."

"Mmm-hmm. Come on, baby girl. Your daddy's acting a wee bit strange tonight." From the living room, she called, "Nice music, by the way. And the table looks lovely."

Was that a snicker in her voice? He *knew* he'd overdone it. Good thing he'd talked himself out of the tie. For good measure, he unbuttoned his shirt cuffs and rolled them halfway up his forearms. Maybe he should tousle his hair a bit so it didn't look like he'd plastered it with styling spray. How did his identical twin brother manage looking good without all the extra prep? Clean country living, no doubt. Samuel really needed to get out of the barn office more often and embrace his inner cowboy.

When Sophie's formula had warmed, he carried it to Joella. "Dinner should be ready about the time she finishes."

Taking the bottle, she offered it to the baby. "Here you go, sweetheart." Without looking at Samuel, she said, "You can mix the dressing and croutons into the salad if you want."

"Uh, okay." Guess he wasn't needed here.

The kitchen timer dinged. He set the lasagna on a trivet, then slid a loaf of garlic bread into the oven to bake while he prepared the salad.

A few minutes later, Joella came in with Sophie propped on her shoulder. "Just got a lovely burp. She should be happy and comfortable now. Shall I put her in her bouncy seat near the table?"

"That'd be great. I'll be right out with dinner."

They kept the conversation light while they ate, and Sophie entertained them with gurgles and smiles. Afterward, Samuel started a pot of decaf, and while he cleared away the dinner plates, Joella sliced the pie. By then, Sophie was getting sleepy, so Samuel took her to the nursery to change her diaper and tuck her into her sleep sack.

Rocking her in his arms, he hummed softly along with the romantic ballad wafting from the living room. As Sophie relaxed into sleep, he laid her in the crib. "Guess I'm on my own now," he whispered, leaning over to kiss her forehead. "Wish me well, okay?"

He turned to find Joella wearing a crooked grin as she watched him from the doorway. "All this whispering between you two. Why do I get the feeling you and your daughter are scheming behind my back?"

"Us? Scheme?" He pretended to look affronted. Brushing past her, he said, "I'm ready for dessert. How about you?" Truth be told, he'd rather taste those lips again.

Easy, fella. If this evening goes as planned, you'll get your chance.

Seated together on the sofa a few minutes later, they nibbled pecan pie and sipped cinnamon-flavored decaf coffee.

After setting her empty plate next to his on the coffee table, Joella shifted slightly to face him. "Have you and your family had any more thoughts about your grandfather?"

"We have." He took her hand and wove his fingers through hers. "When you and I talked yesterday, you planted the seed for some very promising ideas."

"Really? I don't remember saying all that much that could be helpful."

"Mainly, it was your reminder about not trying to face the situation alone. You saw how many old friends showed up for Tito's birthday. Many of them are local, and I doubt it would take much persuasion to get them to commit to a visiting schedule. Even a couple of hours a day would give my parents a break, and that way, we could keep Tito in his own home for as long as possible."

"That's a wonderful plan. The familiarity of friends will also help him hold on to his memories." Looking away, Joella sniffed. "I can't help but wonder how much longer my mother would have lasted if she hadn't withdrawn from the friends who knew her best."

"Jo-Jo..." He released her hand and then slid his arm around her shoulder. With his other hand, he gently turned her head until she met his gaze. "I want to be there for you. Always."

She cast him a tender smile. "I'd like to show you something. Wait right here."

Confused, he watched as she went to the door and disappeared onto the landing before returning with a large shopping bag. She brought the bag to the sofa and set it on the floor at their feet. Reaching inside, she withdrew a lacquered rectangular box about a foot long and six inches deep, with brass hinges and a decorative latch.

"My dad's hobby was woodworking, and he made this for my mom. He called it her Memory Keeper." After a moment's hesitation, she eased open the lid to reveal a hodgepodge of mementos—photos, letters, greeting cards, seashells and shiny stones, random small knickknacks and vacation souvenirs.

Samuel examined a Grand Canyon refrigerator magnet, then a thumb-size replica of a lighthouse. Joella showed him a photograph of a laughing couple on a rocky beach, salt spray rising behind them and their hair tangled by the wind. The love in their eyes as they clung to each other couldn't be denied.

With the tip of one finger, Joella traced the design on a glittery anniversary card. "Whenever Mom would start drifting away, Dad would bring out this box, and for a little while he could draw her back again while they relived some of their happiest memories."

"What an amazing idea. I need to tell my parents about this for Tito."

"That isn't the only reason I wanted to show it to you." She set the box on the coffee table and then reached into the shopping bag once more. This time, she brought out a newer-looking mahogany-stained box, similar in size to the first one. The lid bore the silhouetted image of a couple holding hands beneath a tree. Next to the tree was an inscription: *The story of us.*

Heart thudding, Samuel touched the words. "Us?"

Without replying, Joella opened the lid. Inside lay a photo taken at Spencer and Lindsey's wedding. It showed Joella and Samuel arm in arm as they followed the newlyweds out of the chapel.

He lifted the photo, only to find another, much older snapshot beneath it. Two teenagers, soaking wet after their kayaks rammed into each other and dumped them out, were laughing so hard they could hardly find their footing to wade out of the river. "Oh, wow, I remember this! You purposely rowed in front of me to keep me from winning the race."

"No, I'm pretty sure *you* rammed into *me*." Joella tapped a fingernail against the picture. "That's why I tipped over first and lost my paddle. See, you're still holding yours."

With an exaggerated eye roll, Samuel smirked. "Fine, have it your way." Come to think of it, he did sort of remember trying to cut her off. Then, swallowing, he grew serious. "One thing I do remember about that day—

it's the first time I realized how big a crush I had on you."

"The feeling was mutual, you know." Her eyes turned smoky. "Why do you think I've kept this picture all these years?"

Voice roughening, he glanced away. "Then I had to ruin everything. I hate what a conceited kid I was."

"Don't, Samuel. It isn't who you are now, and that's all that matters."

"A new creation in Christ—that's what my mother keeps reminding me." He lifted her hand to his lips for a gentle kiss. "And you make me want to be a better person, because what I feel for you now goes a million times deeper than any teenage crush."

She smiled, nothing but love shining from the depths of those beautiful brown eyes.

It was time. Releasing her hand, he gently closed the lid on the memory box and set it behind him on the sofa. "I have something to show you, too. Be right back."

He made a quick trip to his bedroom, then joined her again on the sofa. "My box isn't nearly as big as yours," he said, a tiny hinged case sitting atop his palm, "but it could be the start of many more happy memories…if you'll only say yes."

A twinkle in her eye, she looked at him

askance. "I don't believe I've heard a question yet."

"So I need to do this by the book, do I?" With an exaggerated groan, he slid from the sofa and dropped to one knee in front of her. "Joella Louise James," he said, "woman of my dreams. Will you do me the honor of becoming my wife and a mother to my daughter and the passel of kids I hope we have someday?"

She laughed out loud. "First of all, my middle name is Mary, not Louise. And *passel*? We may need to talk about that."

His heart was nearly pounding out of his chest at the fact that she hadn't outright said no. To marrying him or to having more kids. "Well, I don't think you ever told me your middle name, so I was winging it. But Mary is a beautiful name. And sure, we can table the kids discussion as long as you need to."

"Very well," she said with feigned solemnity. "Show me what's in the box."

"Oh, right." He tipped back the lid to reveal a delicate gold ring set with an aquamarine gem surrounded by tiny diamonds. He looked up at her, his tone mellowing. "This was my grandmother's. Tito gave me his blessing to offer it to you."

Fingers to her lips, she choked on a soft sob. "He did?"

"Yeah, he's decided the way you dote on Sophie makes you pretty special."

"Oh, Samuel, there's nothing in the world I want more than to be your wife and Sophie's mom."

"Then…that's a yes?"

She hesitated only briefly before nodding. "Yes. Yes, I'll marry y—"

He didn't let her finish. The ring box fell to the floor as he scooped her into his arms for a kiss he knew they would both remember for the rest of their lives.

Epilogue

Drawing a shaky breath, Joella looked into the eyes of the man she was about to pledge her life to. "Ready to do this?"

They stood outside the chapel doors on a warm Sunday evening in late June, the sun hovering just above the hills. Samuel clutched her left hand and ran his thumb across the aquamarine stone in his grandmother's ring. "Are you sure? Because I don't want you someday wishing you'd gone all out with the formal church wedding and five hundred guests."

"I am absolutely sure. Small and intimate is exactly what I want."

Yesterday, they'd hosted the wedding of Zach Muñoz and Jenny Thomas, the clients whose booking had given River Bend Events and Wedding Chapel its start. During preparations for the big day, it had occurred to Joella that since the chapel would already be decked out with candles and flowers, why not take advantage and save herself and her hardworking friends the extra effort? When she'd presented her idea to Jenny and Zach, they'd been delighted to leave their decorations in place an extra day for Joella and Samuel.

Now, exhausted after the days leading up to the Thomas-Muñoz wedding but bursting with anticipation, she wanted only to walk down the chapel aisle on Samuel's arm, recite their vows to each other and hear the pastor proclaim those blessed words: *I now pronounce you husband and wife.*

The door opened a crack and Spencer peeked out. "The crowd's growing restless. Y'all coming?"

"Right now." Samuel tucked Joella's hand in the crook of his arm.

Grinning, Spencer opened both doors wide. From inside came a collective gasp, and all heads turned to look their way. The gathering included only those nearest and dearest to them—Samuel's parents and grandfather, Lindsey and Spencer, Audra, Holly and her son, and of course Sophie, cuddled in Lois's arms. Joella had been pleasantly surprised when Samuel told her Arturo would attend. The softening of the old man's heart remained a work in progress, complicated by his dementia, but he'd expressed regret at not being there for Spencer's wedding and insisted he wouldn't miss Samuel's.

Joella, in a simple white calf-length sheath, and Samuel, wearing dark slacks and a crisp white dress shirt open at the collar, strode down the aisle to meet the pastor in front of the altar. Spencer and Lindsey joined them on either side, and the next several minutes passed in a happy blur. Their personal vows and chosen Scripture readings underscored truths Joella intended to cling to from this day forward, especially the verse from Second Timothy: *For God hath not given us the spirit of fear; but of power, and of love, and of a sound mind.*

Their first night as husband and wife began with a romantic dinner for two at the Cadwallader Inn, but since they were both anxious to get home to Sophie and begin their lives together, they stayed only until the next morning. After collecting the baby from Lois—and enduring a good-natured scolding for rushing back so soon—they went upstairs to the apartment.

Samuel paused outside the door. "I'd like to carry my bride across the threshold, but..." Shrugging, he glanced from Joella to the baby in his arms. "Besides, I'm hoping we won't have to call this tiny apartment home for much longer."

"Oh?" Joella arched her brow. "Does this have anything to do with the *passel* of kids you mentioned the night you proposed?"

"My life feels complete just as it is—for now, anyway. No," he continued with a pensive frown, "I just want my family to have something more permanent, a place to call our own. I was thinking of asking my dad if he'd give us some land to build a house, maybe on the other side of the old barn. It's really pretty over there, with trees and a creek—"

"It sounds perfect." She stretched up to kiss him.

They'd talked about many things in recent weeks, including Samuel's ever-increasing contentment in working for his father. He'd told Joella he believed he'd finally found his place in the family business—not that he'd ever be the horseman his father, grandfather and brother were, but being home again had reminded him how much he loved the ranch, and he wanted more than ever to fulfill his role in the Navarro Quarter Horses legacy.

They lingered on the landing, Joella's arm wrapped around his waist and Sophie snuggled between them. "You know," she began, "this whole carry-your-bride-over-the-threshold thing is kind of old-fashioned."

He looked at her askance. "First the no-frills wedding with borrowed decorations, now this? Somehow, I'd always assumed you were a traditionalist."

"About some things, yes." With a quiet sigh, she rested her head against his shoulder. "But I'm learning that if you hold too tightly to your preconceptions, you risk missing out on something even more amazing."

"Like marrying the love of your life?"

"Exactly." Tilting her head, she gazed up at him, her heart feeling like it could burst with happiness. "So what do you say, Mr. Navarro? I can't wait to make more wonderful memories with you, so how about we walk through the door together—you, me and this precious baby girl?"

Eyes filled with the deepest love, he beamed an irresistible smile. "I will gladly walk with you through every door God opens for us for the rest of our lives."

* * * * *

Dear Reader,

Fear is powerful. It's a God-given emotion alerting us that something in our lives is amiss. The threat could be as real as a stalker on a dark street or a cancer diagnosis, or as futile as imagining all the horrible things that *might* happen. As Joella and Samuel discovered, fear of the unknown can be the scariest of all.

Whatever the threat, real or imagined, we can trust absolutely in God's everlasting love and continued presence. God doesn't want fear to control our lives, nor does He want us to shun the support and encouragement of those who love us. If you're dealing with something scary in your life, don't face it alone. Reach out and ask for the help you need.

I hope Samuel and Joella's story inspired you to look deeper into any fears you've been harboring. Let God guide your next steps, and know that He cares.

Thank you for spending time with me in fictional Gabriel Bend, Texas. I love hearing from my readers, so please contact me through my website, www. MyraJohnson.com, where you can also subscribe to my e-newsletter.

Or write to me c/o Love Inspired Books, 195 Broadway, New York, NY 10007.

With prayers and gratitude,
Myra